SET MY HEART ON FIRE

Set My Heart on Fire

A Novel

Izumi Suzuki

Translated by Helen O'Horan

VERSO

London • New York

This English-language edition published by Verso 2024
Copyright © 2023 by Suzuki Azusa
Original Japanese edition published as *Hato ni hi wo tsukete! Dare ga kesuin*
[Ignite (one's) heart! Who will extinguish (it)?] 1996 by BUNYA-Sha Inc.
This English edition is published by arrangement with BUNYA-Sha inc, Tokyo
Translation © Helen O'Horan 2024

1 3 5 7 9 10 8 6 4 2

Verso
UK: 6 Meard Street, London W1F 0EG
US: 388 Atlantic Avenue, Brooklyn, NY 11215
versobooks.com

Verso is the imprint of New Left Books

ISBN-13: 978-1-80429-330-0
ISBN-13: 978-1-80429-332-4 (US EBK)
ISBN-13: 978-1-80429-331-7 (UK EBK)

British Library Cataloguing in Publication Data
A catalogue record for this book is available from the British Library

Library of Congress Cataloging-in-Publication Data

Names: Suzuki, Izumi, 1949–1986, author. | O'Horan, Helen, translator.
Title: Set my heart on fire : a novel / Izumi Suzuki ; translated by Helen
   O'Horan.
Other titles: Hāto ni hi o tsukete! English
Description: London ; New York : Verso, 2024.
Identifiers: LCCN 2024013149 (print) | LCCN 2024013150 (ebook) | ISBN
   9781804293300 (paperback) | ISBN 9781804293324 (ebk)
Subjects: LCGFT: Novels.
Classification: LCC PL861.U9265 H3813 2024 (print) | LCC PL861.U9265
   (ebook) | DDC 895.63/5 – dc23/eng/20240627
LC record available at https://lccn.loc.gov/2024013149
LC ebook record available at https://lccn.loc.gov/2024013150

Typeset in Electra by Hewer Text UK Ltd, Edinburgh
Printed and bound by CPI Group (UK) Ltd, Croydon, CR0 4YY

CONTENTS

1

This Bad Girl

Etsuko was standing at the entrance. She wore a mesh vest dyed red, green and black. A pair of dark slim Lee jeans. Chunky wedge sandals garnished with strange little Chinese tassels. With her arms crossed, glaring into space, she looked like an enraged bird-of-paradise. The image made me smirk.

I only saw her first because I was wearing contact lenses. My eyes stung. I put on an appropriate expression for meeting a friend, adjusted my small satin bag and climbed the wide stone steps. 'Hey, over here.'

The look on her face softened in response. Her wide eyes stood out in the dusk, her skin was lightly tanned. She uncrossed her arms and smiled at me.

'You cut your hair.'

I stroked my unsettling head of thumbnail-length hair.

'Well, I had nothing to do the other night.'

My hair was too fine for it – I used to be fair as a kid. It wouldn't stand up, just wrapped itself neatly around my scalp.

I bought a razor cutter and did it myself. Didn't look in the mirror once till it was done. Managed to shape it by feel alone. Then I dyed it blonde, with some grey and green tints.

'I like your earrings, too,' she said, admiring my small silver stars. I twisted around from side to side to let her take me all in.

'Don't you think it's too short?' I looked back into her eyes, chestnuts in their sockets.

'No, it really suits you. They call it a "skinhead," don't they? The new trend from London. Those radical homosexuals have them sometimes. You're ahead of the curve, Izumi. You've got style.'

Crowds of girls were gathering.

'The group's called Diana. This is only their first gig, you know,' she said. 'Looks like a decent turnout.'

Etsuko pushed on the heavy glass door. She scanned the room. Spotted a colleague, smiled instantly. She stood there chatting like she'd done this a thousand times before. Sometimes she let out a forced laugh. The guy, lanky and dressed up like a Chelsea rocker, cocked his head to one side and nodded along. His polka-dot neckerchief just screamed showbiz dickhead. His speech was full of industry jargon. He took the care to drawl his words. Nervy, I distanced myself from them. I couldn't get used to this kind of scene.

Etsuko turned around. 'All fine, let's go in.' She looked relieved. Free admission for us.

It was still early. We leaned against a wall and had a smoke by ourselves.

'They're a proper rock 'n' roll band from Kawasaki. You don't see that style much nowadays: pompadours, ducktails, leather jackets. They got their first break playing *Ginza Now*. Mickey Curtis called up the TV station before the show had even ended.'

I gave a vague nod. I didn't have a TV, didn't listen to the radio, didn't know anything about any trends out there.

'Everyone's into folk at the moment, though. No real bands about. The groupies were all just dying for it. You can't scream at an acoustic guitar under a spotlight, can you? Then these Diana guys show up. Everyone was *so* ready for them.'

I played with the pendant displayed in the deep-cut neckline of my art-deco dress. It carried an opal stone I'd bought in a half-price sale. Music news meant nothing to me.

'What are you listening to, these days?' Etsuko's question was good-natured.

'This Roxy Music record. There's a woman with blue eye shadow lying on satin bedsheets on the cover. The music sounds all sparky and loose. With all these jerky stops and starts, like a seizure.'

'Ah, yes. Nice, nice.' She'd dropped into music journo mode.

'Plus I found these Green Glass LPs in a second-hand record shop. Stunning guy on the covers! His beauty had such a hold on me that I ended up buying the records. And the music turned out to be good.'

'You mean the kid with the small face and long neck? Freakishly long limbs, abnormally skinny?'

I nodded.

'That's Joel, the half-white guy I've been telling you about. You really hadn't seen him before?'

I shook my head.

'He's famous, darling.' She grabbed my arm firmly. 'More gorgeous than you could ever imagine, right?'

'You see a lot of girlish pretty boys about. But he's got a real man's face, hasn't he? Firm, clear-cut features.' I saw him again in my mind's eye. One glance and I'd never forget what he looked like.

'Which albums did you find?'

'Their second and third. The rhythm and blues one and the rockier blues one. You can really tell he's mixed, can't you? I've never seen such big eyes. The whites practically like oceans around those greenish pupils of his. It's almost scary. Hollow, you know? So alien. Such an empty gaze. As if there's something wrong. He must be a total nutjob.'

'He was in a mental hospital, actually. Went a bit overboard sniffing glue.'

'No surprise.'

'He had a rep as a pretty boy in Yokohama too. Apparently gangs of girls used to ambush him at the gates after school. He had a fanbase even before he'd started playing in bands. But photos have nothing on the real thing. Wait till you see how his colouring changes in person.'

'He changes colour?'

'Depending on the light. He'll be pale as a sheet one moment, olive-skinned the next. I saw him in Roppongi and got his autograph. He was so shy. So quiet. The kind of guy who can't say no if a girl accosts him.'

Etsuko was clued up about everything. I stopped watching TV as a teenager, so I only knew the major-label Group Sounds bands. I remembered hearing Green Glass from a

4

car radio sometime, and thinking they were weird. The lyrics seemed rough for an era saturated with sweet girlish songs by the Tigers or whoever, 'I met my Mary on a lonely rain-filled morning . . .' Meanwhile Green Glass were singing about a short-term fling, this girl fooling around with an American soldier. The performance was tight and rich. And more than anything, fast. It had ferocious momentum.

'Bad boys are way cooler down in Honmoku,' she went on. 'The Tempters barely cut it. Sure, you get gangs in Saitama all kitted out in baggy *sukaman* trousers too – but even the name *sukaman* is short for Yokosuka Mambo, right? Yokosuka, Yokohama . . . if you're after the latest music they're the best places in Japan for it, with the American military bases and everything. The jukeboxes are all in English. Culturally, it's like a colony there. Before Japanese music mags even had a chance to pick up on what songs were hits overseas, Green Glass were already up there playing them on stage.'

Etsuko was getting carried away with her commentary. 'Group Sounds was mostly influenced by British music, right? Almost as if there was some perfect affinity in the air, English fog married with Japanese humidity. But those guys suddenly came out with a very American sound.'

'Because of the US base in Honmoku?'

'That, but also their own backgrounds. Apart from the front-man, they were all either foreign or mixed.'

'The vocalist is the short guy, right?'

'He's not short. Joel's just too tall. Apparently mixed kids got bullied even in Yokohama. People lobbed stones at them,

5

stuff like that. Joel once said all he could remember from his childhood was crying in Harbour View Park every day.'

'Little wonder. No hiding for a halfie.' I picked at the skin on my lips.

'But once he got a bit older, girls started going wild for the very same thing that got him bullied before. Either way, he's always been singled out. Tragic, isn't it?'

'Really?' For me, that's just the way of the world. But here was Etsuko, outraged. Would she even be interested if Joel wasn't so good-looking?

'I would have been his friend if I'd met him when I was a kid.' She seemed genuinely disappointed about missing her chance. 'I would've kept quiet and stared. I mean, he's like a mannequin. It's spooky. I might've made fun of him myself. I was a late bloomer.' Etsuko craned her neck forward. 'When was your first time?'

'Eighteen.'

'Earlier than me.' She shook her head, annoyed. I guess she'd taken a quick glance back at her own sex life.

I stared intently at Etsuko's face. She resembled a gaudier Yoko Ono. She certainly made a strong impression, but had zero sex appeal. Being different and less than pretty wasn't generally a good formula.

'Men, you know . . .' Then she pulled herself together. Took a drag on her cigarette, got back on topic. 'The important thing is that Green Glass were Japan's first blues band. When they played Paul Butterfield or Blues Project songs, their versions were *way* darker than the originals.'

'Maybe they had a downright gloomy outlook on life.' I smiled.

'Then the proggy stuff took over at the end. They played the outdoor concert hall in Hibiya. That's about as far as they kept up with what was happening abroad. They split up for good in seventy-one. Joel had left by then, though.'

Etsuko knew everything. She'd started working as a journalist because she was obsessed with the Tigers and decided she wanted to talk on an equal footing with 'those kinds of people'. She'd come all the way from Kyushu. It must have taken some guts.

She saw a stumpy arrow on the wall. Nodding, she opened the soundproofed door. I followed her like I was retarded. She skirted along the wall and found some seats at the front.

'There's fine,' she said, pointing. 'Go and sit down.'

I did as I was told.

'They'll be starting soon. Stay here, won't you? D'you want a drink? Let me fetch something for you.'

Why was she being so nice? I shook my head like a child.

'No. Don't want anything.'

'Okay then, sit tight.' Etsuko left through a side door.

The curtain rose. Four band members in black leather jackets and trousers stood there looking slightly stiff. Delighted squeals from the audience. Me, I missed the cue to shriek. I wasn't used to these places.

They started up with energy. The sound was harsh and relentless. The crowd applauded. The band's gestures grew more dramatic with every number. Hands above heads, leaping, clapping. Some fans were up on their feet, too. Etsuko returned close to the last song. Several encores seemed likely, though. We both went out into the corridor before the lights went up.

Etsuko sank languorously onto a sofa. She probably wanted to make it clear that we were in a different league to the manic fangirls leaving the show. She pressed a finger into her cheek, looking smug. 'They did alright, didn't they?'

I had no idea. This was the first time I'd seen them. I tried hard to come up with some original feedback. 'I was surprised how the bassist kept coming out to the front. I just assumed rhythm players kept going steadily in the background.'

'He's the band leader, you know. He writes the songs. Bit of an exhibitionist. It's all for show, of course. Well, I suppose that's how they got their break. He grew up without his mum, apparently, in absolute poverty. So he swore he'd become famous. Foo, though – he's a gentle, quiet guy.' Etsuko was dating Foo, the nineteen-year-old lead guitarist.

'So, tonight was a success. But I guess that could mean we'll be seeing less of each other.'

She took her imported menthol cigarette out of her mouth and stared ahead. Before I could ask anything she burst out: 'It's fine, men are just like that.' Like what? I didn't know. Or pretended not to know. She turned to face me. 'You're twenty-three, right?'

'Yeah.'

'You'll understand when you're my age. Single at twenty-seven. People don't look at me. I can't just *smile* sweetly at men. You should remember this. You're too nice. You're selling yourself short. All you have to do is ignore them. Men are only passionate at the start.'

That wasn't my experience. I'd always be the one to get obsessed when I first met someone. Then he'd be ignited by

8

my fire. He'd decide we should start going steady. And just about then, every time, a new man would magically appear. It's not nice to admit it, but I'd then have zero problem betraying the first one.

I ran at a different tempo to most of my lovers. By no means was I flippant. I'd pour highly concentrated, strong, intense feelings into a man. I'm sure it looked very fervent and emotional. I think it is. But there's an affected quality to my affection.

I'm passionate, of course. Passion is something that occurs naturally. Yet when the time comes, I make it occur artificially. That seems different to ordinary enthusiasm. Distorted. There's something forced and unnatural about it. I can cool it down at will. For me there's little distance between loving and hating someone. You'd think I had extensive acting experience. My true self and my performed self, when I get them well mixed up, are indistinguishable from each other.

I had to stop sprinting about, or no one would love me. But no one would love me anyway. No person would do me that favour. That's a given. Who could be honest with a monstrous woman like me? No man on this planet. He can't exist. That's a fact. I'd turned this idea into a strange little sort of conviction.

'Men are just their libidos!' Etsuko was being assertive.

I made an ambivalent sound in response. I never care. So long as he holds me.

'It's true!' she insisted.

I made an effort to listen to her opinions earnestly. I didn't pretend to agree, though. I knew I was far more experienced than her, both quantitively and qualitatively.

9

'Simple as.' Furnishing her point, she stubbed out her cigarette. The filter crumpled into the white ash carpeting the metal ashtray. She stood up. 'Let's go to the green room.'

We went up and down some iron stairs. Etsuko took a breath outside the door. Her casual pose in place, she knocked.

The room stank of sweat. The frontman was bent over fixing his hair.

'Hey,' he said, turning round. He left his silver comb by the mirror. He looked elderly here. Lots of wrinkles. The bottom half of his face hung funny and twisted.

'You were great.' Etsuko reached out a hand.

'Cheers.' The band leader shook her hand firmly.

'This is my friend, Izumi.'

'Nice to meet you.' He held out his hand to me and I hastily shook it.

Etsuko introduced the other three members. I quickly sized them up, as per. The drummer was a shortie. The rhythm guitarist had an angular face. Etsuko's guy was nothing special, but he was slightly better than the rest of the line-up. I was able to rank boys by their looks so swiftly by then that it felt like a sort of arcane skill. They nodded and said the usual hellos.

'We'll be keeping an eye out for you.' Etsuko spoke as cheerfully as she could. To salvage the situation. As self-encouragement. Everyone nodded again and said whatever they said.

The night had thickened outside.

Scatterings of neon lights softly stained the rich dark.

It was the same night. The same night several times, all overlapping at once. A thousand nights in the same place at the same time, all distinct from one another. Each delineated, no relation whatsoever to any other. But also, unaware, resonating among themselves. This single, particular night.

As if an echo-chamber effect pedal had been plugged into time. Like the one The Happenings Four use in their 'Alligator Boogaloo' cover: *Boogaloo-loo-loo-loo* . . . It leaves a trembling, trailing tail and the sound comes back, bit by bit.

The reverb of this night *in this time* within this partitioned space continues endlessly. It has absolutely no influence on other times. The sad echo of the *loo-loo-loo-loo* builds up to become water pressure and my skin can hear it.

Messy and clear. Glib and shallow. An extremely artificial beauty, as in a dream. Cold and curt enough to set my heart racing.

'Come to the café. I can't stay long though.'

Etsuko seemed to be trying to soothe her nerves. She'd probably expected a warmer welcome in the dressing room.

'Is it about work?' I pretended not to know.

'It's a meeting. At this time! Honestly. I have to be up early tomorrow as well. Got six pages to write before noon. Two interviews, then another meeting.' She also had to follow around a rising songwriter who, rumour had it, was soon set to tie the knot.

'I'm free all the time,' I said, smiling.

'Nice for some.' She shot me a guarded look.

'It's always the same day, over and over. And here I am going out chasing good times like a maniac. There's nothing else to do. I've got to have fun, I no longer have a choice. It's an obsessive compulsion. I'm uneasy, unsettled, unsteady. But I feel like it'd be even scarier if I stopped.'

'It remains a mystery to me, how you live.'

'I do work three days a month.' I grinned.

'It amazes me how calm you are about it.'

She honestly seemed to admire me.

But the same night will continue on. Today is just yesterday, continued. Tomorrow is just today, continued. Day breaks, night falls, day breaks. Night probably falls again. The little details differ, sure. But for the most part, everything is pretty much the same, and I feel neither more nor less sluggish today than I did last Thursday. I am sluggish. But still compelled to dance. Provided there's some variety to the music.

I'm trapped inside an invisible cage, you see. I can't leave it. I feel so hollow and futile it makes me sick. It's easy, though.

'You're alright, you are.' Etsuko's compliment sounded bitter.

The windowed café was fitted out with an antique woodgrain which had started to be popular.

Etsuko ordered a coffee and lit up a cigarette out of habit. She took a drag, then suddenly grimaced.

'Ugh, no.' Her voice was hoarse.

'My stomach's surprisingly okay,' I told her. 'Mamy Blue' was playing.

'This was a hit last year, wasn't it?' I asked. Etsuko's mind seemed elsewhere. I went on: 'Don't Japanese people love poppy western songs, like "In the Year 2525" and "The Train".'

How could I spew out such nonsense? It just flows out of my mouth. As long as it has a beat. The meaning is secondary. The main concern is tempo and rhythm. Aside from that, it's just whatever comes out of my mouth.

Our coffee and ice creams arrived.

'Vanilla Fudge,' I said.

' "You Keep Me Hangin' On",' Etsuko supplied.

An American psych rock band and one of their best-known songs. They hardly played any original material. I guess they were like a western Group Sounds band. Not dissimilar to the Jaguars. Still, I liked their name. I prefer vanilla over chocolate or strawberry, after all.

'Why don't you do some modelling?'

'I stopped doing that after three months, when I was twenty.' Which wasn't really a reason not to do it again. But I couldn't be bothered to explain further. I'd blithely leave things half-baked like that, so long as no one picked up on it.

'They say modelling isn't as easy as it looks, don't they? Once you actually try it. I hear it's quite tough work.'

'Everyone loves saying that. To keep the profession sacred or something, I dunno. But let me tell you, it's the easiest fucking work out there. It's so lax. Honestly.'

'Well, you just had the knack, then. Don't the guys harass you on jobs like that?'

'God, no, I don't sleep with my business interests. I pick up men for that off the street.'

'That's cool.'

Etsuko was gazing into her cup. What was cool? Was she trying to be bold and easy like me?

What a frigid woman. Sorry to think it, but still. Frigid ones do have a certain personality. They come out with these catchphrases like, 'Who gives a shit about men?' They don't leave themselves any wriggle room. They're distant and indifferent. Stiff, rigid ways of thinking about things. Spend too long with a woman like that and you'll be shattered by the end of it. Me? I do give a shit. Maybe too much, but that's another issue.

The waiter killing time at the counter changed the channel on the TV. A male singer, screaming 'Go ahead!' It was about a long-haired girl's heartbreak. The third and best-selling single by Green Glass. Either 1967 or 1968. Felt like aeons ago.

'You know, the band didn't want to do this song because it sounded so old and fusty. Landi, the lead guitarist, he liked new stuff. He was the first person in Japan to get a fuzzbox. Everyone was still on a roll from their debut, which is why it's so full-on.'

'Landi, the blues guitarist from Chinatown? He's the best Group Sounds player, right?'

'Right. There's Yamaguchi Fujio from the Dynamites, too, though he only later suddenly got really good, after obsessing over Mike Bloomfield. Chinese Landi, well, he was a knock-out from the start. Hard to forget that insistent guitar, it sticks like glue. He works at a Chinese restaurant now, apparently.'

Etsuko's tough-woman stance only lets up a little when having chats like this.

'It was better before all the Anpo stuff. So showy, loud and all over the place. What a boring time we're in now. Rock music's got so tame since the seventies started.'

More grievances. Still, although I wasn't sad about it myself, I did share her opinion. So I suddenly said, 'Grace Slick was so stunning.'

'Mmm, from Jefferson Airplane.' Etsuko let her gaze wander upwards.

'Do you ever feel like you've aged really quickly? I feel like an old lady already.' I leaned forward. I wondered whether it was just me who felt this, or if it was something about our era.

'Yes, I do.' Etsuko nodded.

'Maybe because music's dropped the psychedelia.'

'That stuff did have a lot of youth about it. Well, I'm the older one, so I guess I got to feel young like that for a little longer than you did.' Etsuko smiled faintly.

Just one year longer, if we take 1970 as the cut-off. I was born in 1949, you see, and left home at twenty.

'I'll make up for it,' I said.

'In that case you're best off hanging out with Joel. If you could, that is. Of course we can't really. I mean, he's a living embodiment of the late sixties. Probably the guy who most reflects the era. He's always been a big star, and I'm not just talking about his current actual fame. He's just always had that kind of personality. Once Green Glass made it, he couldn't be bothered anymore. He's always taking time off. Doesn't give a reason. Just says, "Taking a day off today," and naps at home, won't come out unless the manager goes to get him. "Taking a day off today." Isn't that great?' Etsuko laughed and squeezed my hand.

'It's great.'

'No other band would play with a member short. But they'd have someone else stand in on bass and it'd be terrible. It sort of felt like he was defying us. Like he was saying, you lot just don't get my art. At the time I used to haunt the jazz cafés, hoping to run into him. So it hit me pretty hard.'

'Has he just given up?'

'He has now. Probably,' she said quietly.

'Since when?'

'Since he was nineteen, I guess. Scary, isn't it. He turned into such a meek, quiet person. At that age. He's a year older than you. He used to wave these big knives about, you know? Hurl his guitar at the audience. Three months after their debut, the band were at the Nichigeki for the Western Carnival and Joel played a bass solo that lasted a full fifteen minutes. No one had seen anything like it, they were so shocked. The critics were all calling him a genius. He just shrugged and chewed his gum. That was probably the high point of his entire life. At eighteen years old.'

'He reached the top, then it was all downhill from there.'

'In terms of the music, yes. And his motivation. But their popularity had been flagging . . . Now, he's become a legend.'

Yes, of course. We had so many *legendary* people and places back then (we were talking in 1973). A certain person walking down a certain street would cause a scandal. An unbelievable time.

I'm chasing after vanished fantasies. The beautiful, the flashy, the suave, the curious, the feel-good, anything. Be it fake or counterfeit or whatever.

'You okay for time?' I asked.

'I should go,' Etsuko said, taking the bill. 'I'll pay. I invited you.'

We waited for her change at the till. 'Actually,' she said, 'I just remembered. You know Foo, the lead guitarist from the band. He said he's coming over to mine tonight. He's broke, he needs some cash.'

I finally made it back home. I was always shattered, but that day it was particularly bad. I thought I might collapse on the street.

I threw myself on the bed and laid there motionless, like a crumpled rag.

My breathing was agitated. Veins stood out around my temples. I could hear the blood thumping so hard it hurt. It even pulsed in my wrists. The backs of my knees. My hips. Blood, flowing. I felt it clearly all over.

My silky-smooth blood. Thin, empty blood. It wasn't thick enough, probably because I never ate my greens. Not enough iron or vitamin E. My little heart was running flat out.

The meds would kill me before long. Each night I gave myself up to those white pills. Or into the arms of a man. I just wanted to be held by something. Taken in. I couldn't tell what pleasure was anymore. At first you get high to feel good or check out. Then, once you're using regularly, it stops feeling good. Your brain can't check out, it doesn't get you there. But you don't learn, you keep taking it just to escape the withdrawal. To forget the chilling despair you feel when you sober up.

Time to quit.

I decided to quit fairly flippantly. Then told myself it was 'just for a while' and 'just for the time being'. If push came to shove, I could always get hold of whatever I wanted: bromisoval, nitrazepam ... Recently I'd even managed to get hold of methaqualone, for God's sake, that relic from the ancient past.

A man was the healthier choice. Pleasure from drugs was passive, but with sex it was something more active and distinct. I loved being treated gently and caressed. I liked the game, the back and forth. I also didn't mind falling for them occasionally. Men were harmless compared to drugs, I reckoned. So long as I didn't get pregnant.

I steadied my breathing and got up carefully, mindful of feeling dizzy. I sat up on the bed and let out another deep breath. My mind partly blacked out. The darkness seemed to seep from the rear of my head.

I took off my tights and put them in the laundry basket. I felt faint. I dropped to the kitchen floor, unable to help myself. If it weren't for the smell of slowly rotting vegetables down there, I'd have stayed put. I got up. I resolved to eat a rich and varied diet, starting tomorrow. I took off my panties and threw them in the basket too.

I went back to the bed and took off my dress and bra. I lay down stark naked. Etsuko had told me the name of Diana's manager. Right, here goes.

I called directory assistance and got the phone number. When I got through, the lead guitarist hadn't returned yet. I left a message asking him to call me back.

I put on a pair of white lace knickers and a fancy bra and rallied myself. *Volume Two* by Green Glass on the record player.

On came their version of 'Shotgun', a song made popular by Vanilla Fudge (though the original was by Junior Walker and the All Stars on Motown). Such a high-energy track. I guess they got some girls in from an American school to do all the

screaming in the background. The members introduce themselves halfway through: Joel shouts his name out like a diligent
schoolboy while Landi plays it cool, showing off his English
pronunciation. Each member feels totally unconnected to the
next.

My player was pretty cheap, but I could still hear the bass
properly. Or maybe Green Glass just used more prominent
bass than other Japanese bands. So what if you listened to the
record on good speakers? Surely you'd only hear the bass and
nothing else. It was almost too much. Some guitarists have a
gift for playing ultra-fast, but Joel did the same on bass. He
played fast, always. Leaving no gaps. Making melody on a
rhythm instrument.

So that's him, I thought, inspecting the photos on the album
sleeve. They'd shot the cover at the Heian Jingu shrine. Five
guys standing around a red column. Hats off to their record
label. Who'd ever match a band from Honmoku with a temple
in Kyoto?

On the back of the sleeve, the five stood lined up next to
each other, lit from behind. It was rare to see a band whose
members were so different in height and proportions. They
were like specimens in a human zoo.

Joel was wearing a psychedelic T-shirt. He looked almost two
metres tall and would weigh no more than fifty-odd kilos. His
legs were astonishingly long. I wouldn't want to stand beside
someone like him if I were a man.

The next one who stood out was Landi, the lead guitarist.
This band's looks really matched up to their talent. Except for
the plump guy on keys. Chinese Landi seemed pretty suave.

You could sense his discerning taste from his neckerchief and the way his leather waistcoat was unbuttoned. There was a balance between his protruding lower lip and his long, tapering eyes. Lechy and erotic.

I see. So these guys had their moment too. I propped the sleeve against the wall.

The phone rang. A timid-sounding boy was on the other end. It was Diana's lead guitarist.

'Come round to mine,' I told him.

'Can I?' He seemed to be thinking something over, but not too deeply. 'It'll be pretty late.'

'That's okay. Whenever's fine.' I didn't want to take any drugs that night, after all, so this worked nicely.

'Where's your place?'

'Yoyogi-Uehara.'

'Okay, I'll be there about two o'clock. Will a taxi cost much?'

I explained further. 'It's close to Shibuya.'

'Got it.' He put the phone down. He'd left the conversation, but his nineteen-year-old bewilderment lingered for a while.

The first side of the album finished. I turned the record over. Most of the songs were in English. Not only the covers but the originals too. Maybe coming from a place like Honmoku did that to you. I washed my face while listening to the music. Since someone was coming over, I had to put some clothes on. Even if I'd be taking them straight off again.

I leaned into the closet beside my bed and picked out a thirties-style salmon-pink tricot suit. It was trashy and obscene, glittery, a total mess. I'd been into dressing disgracefully ever since I saw *Bonnie and Clyde*. I knew I couldn't be sweet or beautiful, so I emphasised the sordid, raunchy looks I'd been born with.

I got dressed and started doing my makeup. Fake eyelashes, no question. The album had finished playing. I yanked the arm of the player before it jumped back to the start. It made a harsh sound so perhaps I damaged the record.

Hope I'm in for a good time, I thought. Even if it's just for tonight.

The most important thing to me was satisfying immediate sensual desires. Most men, even if they played around a bit, tried to live in a forward-thinking, measured way. I found it so terribly boring. No more, no more. Done with all that. I'd never dated a proper nine-to-fiver, but even those art-adjacent free-lancers had nothing special going on. Musicians, only musicians, would do for me. Theirs was the most sensual, carnal profession, after all. I boiled the kettle and made some tea.

I dropped the needle back on the fourth track of the first side, 'Money'. Chinese Landi was singing. He was much better than the lead vocalist. Somewhere between singing and talking. Speeding along by himself. Bags of confidence. Doing what he felt like. Mostly ad-libbing the lyrics, which were nothing like the liner notes. His voice sounded strange: shrill, sweet, weirdly metallic. As if it had passed through some machine. But they didn't have effects like that back in those Group Sounds days. It's no big deal now, of course. Dry and light. Dehumanised, robotic. Sexy but not at all alluring. It's too good. He's so relaxed that the backing vocals sound hurried and stressed. Diligently chanting 'What I want' on repeat, trying to keep up with him. The only break is the 'can' in 'I

21

can use'. For a split second his voice catches and pitches up like a squeaky rub on a glass. It's the only bit of falsetto before he returns to usual.

Shivering with pleasure, I spilled some tea on my lap. I jumped up but held my hand still to stop the teacup from tipping further over. By the time I'd mopped myself with a tissue the song had rolled to its end.

I'd won a tabletop clock at the pachinko parlour. It read just past one o'clock.

I lay on the bed in my dress and smoked a cigarette. I wanted to see Joel in the flesh. How did he talk? What sort of gestures did he make? From his appearance he seemed a cold fish. The look on his face suggested he was holed up in his own desolate realm and didn't give a fig about the rest of the world.

Guys on drugs were usually cold toward other people. Drugs are fundamentally a solo pursuit, after all. Your perception goes hazy, your senses dull, you care less about the rest.

Drinkers, well, I couldn't stand them. Far too clingy. Alcohol was about everyone doing it together and opening up to each other. I just didn't think it was so vital to talk that freely with people.

I could manage a bottle, but I hated the taste. It was so uncomfortable feeling full and getting all hot. I'd always get a headache after my fifth drink, too, which I didn't enjoy. If alcohol were a pill I'd go on forever, I thought – then I caught myself. My mind was creeping toward the drugs. I had to be careful not to reach for the slender box. I'd bought three packs of Optalidon that afternoon.

I didn't want to think about those cute little pink pills, not if I could help it. As soon as I picture them in my mind I start craving to see them in the flesh. And once they were in my hand I'd probably push one out of its blister pack. Soon ten would have popped out and a whole day would be gone. Even if I woke up, my brain would be blank and my body inert.

I preferred drugs because they were chemical. I wanted their world of artificial, phoney intoxication. A cool, impersonal inebriation.

Nothing for twenty minutes. I'd have premonitions in the meantime. Then a vague, dim wave would approach. Just when I started dozing off idly, I'd suddenly plunge in. Who could forget that terrifying intoxication?

I wondered what my guest might be up to right now. If he didn't come, I'd take the painkillers.

There was a knock on the door. A rather timid one. I got up to answer. Well, I thought, no need for the meds now. Foo was holding his guitar case. He hadn't changed out of his stage outfit.

'Come in.'

His oddly long eyes glistened faintly.

2

I'm Your Puppet

I arrived at a friend's place. I jumped into his empty bed and kicked my legs about.

'I've been summoned.'

'She twigged?' This pal was a comic-strip artist. He lifted his face from his tilted drafting desk. 'I did say you should have been sneakier.'

'But these things always come out of the woodwork anyway. Even if it just happens once or twice.' I pretended I was swimming on the bed.

'How much have you been seeing each other?' He was deftly cutting up tracing paper.

'For the past month and a half. He plays a gig on Saturdays and comes over afterwards.'

'He's seen you both on the same night before, right?' He was annoyingly cool about it.

'Yeah. Twice, I think. He borrowed money from Etsuko and spent it on a taxi to mine.'

'Cheeky scamp. A nineteen-year-old playing two older women.' He taped some tracing paper over a drawing.

'Uh-huh. Some would call it shameless.' I looked up. Some, but not me.

'So this lead guitarist boy's decided to pack it in with Etsuko.' He slipped his work into a large envelope.

'Seems like it. She started to suspect something after all.'

'If it was me, I'd keep seeing the pair of you for a while. You've got the energy for it at nineteen.' This pal was twenty-one.

'But they're doing all this publicity at the moment, he's busy.' It sounded almost like I was covering for Foo.

'Actually, I did see Diana on TV. They really gave it something. Is he the meek-looking one with a Stratocaster? The one playing the white guitar?' He swivelled his chair to face me.

'Fender, two hundred and ten thousand yen. He saved his wages to buy it. Told me you can become a pro if you practice for six months.'

'I'm more of a Gibson man myself. I mean, the Green Glass guitarist used an SG. I guess different Fenders sound different, too. You've got Telecasters, Stratocasters . . . The Tele's nice and tight. Stratocaster's more bluesy.'

He took out a Hope cigarette and a little sleeve of cardboard matches.

'God, what should I do!' I lay back and writhed about on the bed.

'You just never think ahead.' He plucked off a match and lit his cigarette. 'Oh no, I just set my Hope on fire!'

'Look, if it works out in the end, it's all good to me. I take it as it comes.'

'Well then, all sorted.' He laughed, teasing me.

'Except that later it develops into trouble.'

'To me it just looks like you're baiting bother. You're seeking it. You like it, the commotion, the fuss.'

'I don't even understand it myself.'

'You've got guts, I'll give you that. I'm too repressed. I'm a wimp, I could never do what you do. You were born destructive. You're drawn to the bad, you follow it compulsively.'

'Listen, it's at three o'clock. What should I do?' Etsuko told me to be at a café near Shinjuku station. In a rock-hard voice, needless to say.

'First of all, I've got to eat. I've been up all night and haven't had a thing.' He stood up and stretched, fished out a small note and some change. 'Well, I'll get paid once I take these drawings in. I could eat a goddam horse.'

I offered, without thinking, to fetch some ingredients and cook something.

'What? You can cook?' He paused. 'Wait, you did make tempura last time I was at your place. You don't look the type at all, it's totally at odds with your demeanour. Easy to forget.'

'I made this outfit myself, too.'

'You should make more of these skills in front of men, you know.'

'What, let them know I'm domesticated? But I hate housework. I only do it when I have to.'

'Yeah, actually, being really good at cooking or making clothes usually means you're not a homely type. Plenty of domestic women can't do sod all either. The girl I was seeing until recently was like that. She was so psychologically stingy.

Hoarded and saved everything. She remembered every single thing I did, every single place I went. Ask her what happened on our third date or whatever and she'd give an abnormally detailed account, compare me then to how I am now. She made a note of every last damn detail. It's a form of control.'

He stood up and went to the porch to put some trainers on.

'Why did you break up with her?'

'She hoarded and saved too much fat in her body.'

Once he'd worked his heels in, he tightened the laces. He opened the door and turned back around, laughing.

'Accumulating stuff seems to be important to women like that.'

I put on my high-heeled sandals while he waited outside. It was a clear, bright morning. Light coated everything like a powder. The greens were rich.

'This girl I'm seeing at the moment is quite clever. But not like an intellectual. That lot only understand the world through knowledge, right? But this one's really intuitive, she uses her senses. Got both her brain and her body switched on.'

'Is she a good person?' We linked arms.

'I think so, I don't know. She's a total egomaniac, though. Really selfish. It's a bit shocking. But at her core she's honest, no funny business.'

'And she's a looker?'

'Yeah, she is. You know how you get some ugly ones who just seem beyond help, their hearts totally warped by inferiority complexes or something.'

'I've got this theory. Beautiful people have beautiful hearts. Once I decided to stop judging people by their looks and ended up dating a guy with stunted legs.'

'Like me, you mean?' He laughed.

'Look, you're short, so everything's in proportion. This guy was about ten centimetres taller than me, but we had the same length legs.'

'Should I take that as a compliment?'

'Come on. Anyway, whenever we met, he'd say stuff like, "I've got such a bad figure." Honestly I wanted to agree with him, right? It was true. But I had to say no, it's not bad, you know, reassure him in spite of myself. It happened every single time. "How ugly is my face," blah blah. He expected me to deny it. Relied on me to encourage him. In the end I just got sick of it, and told him that everything he said about himself was true.'

He laughed out loud. 'But once you've said it, that really throws a spanner in the works. The truth's suddenly out. Your entire history together gets turned over. What did he do?'

'He just stood there, didn't say a word.'

'I'm sure. But those sorts are weirdly persistent. I bet he called you over and over afterwards, am I right?'

'He announced to me that he'd found someone new. God, this guitarist boy is far better.'

'Quick to compare, aren't you?'

'Don't you do that too?'

'Yeah, I suppose I do. Yes. But I cover it up, I don't tell people about it.'

'Maybe I'm just a bad person then.'

'You're not a bad person, you're just ruthless.' He angled his head towards mine and laughed.

We turned a corner and I asked, 'What do you want to eat?'

'Not bread, not noodles. I don't have a rice cooker, though. So not rice either.'

'You can cook rice in a saucepan, that's what I do. I'll buy you some rice. How about grilled fish? We need tofu and soft seaweed for the miso soup. And spinach for a side dish.'

'Where's all this kindness coming from? Do you get cosy with people you're not dating?'

'I'm like this with everyone. Apart from people I don't like.'

'Even with the guy you're seeing?'

'Yeah. And I'm so pushy about it, I even get sick of myself.'

'I'm petrified you'll have a sudden change of heart. I can't predict that with you. Why don't you keep all that kindness just for me?'

'A cold-hearted guy like you would get fed up if you always saw me like this. We're good as we are.'

'Maybe, maybe.'

It took me half an hour to get everything ready to serve.

'That was quick. You cut any corners?'

He laid the table. We sat facing each other like newly-weds. I scooped up a big helping of the rice as it was still settling.

'Wonder what it'd be like being married to you,' he said.

'Listen. You don't lie to friends, right? But you need to deceive each other if you're going to be lovers.'

'Even with me?' he asked.

'That's why we'll never be together. Where's the fun if you understand each other and feel at peace right from the start? I'll marry someone I can conduct psychological warfare with.

I've known that since my first year at high school. Ever since I read *Who's Afraid of Virginia Woolf?*'

'You're a romantic. But not in the way givrls usually are.'

'I do want to fall in love and get married, though.'

'You're joking,' he said, then turned serious. 'I reckon you are a girly girl, after all.'

I didn't say anything.

He looked up. 'This lead guitar guy, does he treat you well?'

'Very.'

'I can't shake the feeling that you're tricking some young kid. Why is that? Usually with women it's either the guy making her do something or she does something for his sake, right? Then she cries about it afterwards.'

'I cry, too.' I reached for his empty rice bowl. 'Got an appetite, haven't you?'

'I'm pretty sure you cry only after you've judged it's crying that'll have the most effect.'

I thought through an idea, then put it into words. 'It's a waste of time to try and understand men. Lots of women say they know everything about their man, understand him so totally that they just have to be by his side forever. They feel reassured. But that's when men run away. It's a very arrogant mindset.'

'Because a person can only understand what's within their own capacities,' he said. 'Misunderstanding is the basis of communication, after all.'

'That's why it's about tricking one another,' I said. 'Though maybe it's strange to call it that.'

'Listen,' he began, 'I want to come with you later, but I need to get some sleep after taking this to the publisher. Don't think I can last much longer than noon.'

I pouted. 'Okay, fine.'

He tried making up for it. 'What happened with the cameraman you were seeing till recently?'

'I called it off.'

I'd have to go to where I'd been summoned, alone. I felt the shakes coming on.

'How come?'

'He's just a plain old idiot. Couldn't be arsed chatting with him, pissed me right off.'

'Just a plain old idiot!' He chuckled. I glared at him. He kept up his good-mood sham. 'In that case, same with a plain old womaniser. A lost cause, unless there's something else going on.'

I kept quiet and ingested a large quantity of food.

'Did you treat him to the talk?'

'Yes. The theme was "it's for your sake".'

'No one breaks up with someone for the other's sake.'

'I know. But it was good enough.'

'Your break-up talks come in grades too. Standard, advanced, super-advanced . . .'

'Got to tailor it to the guy. I had a break-up fight with this one boy who was preparing for his entrance exams and he ended up failing. Serves him right, he wasn't smart enough anyway.'

'Ruthless.'

'He did have long legs, though.'

Speaking of which. Joel.

31

'Nothing special face-wise?' he asked.

'Nope.'

Those wide, green eyes.

'Actually, I reckon you're quite psychologically involved,' he said.

'What do you mean, "actually"?'

'Well, your behaviour makes you seem very carnal. But things are always psychological for women, in one way or another. Even when it seems trivial from the outside.'

He finished eating. I took the dishes to the sink.

'Wow, you're doing the washing up too? Listen, I'll pay you back for this sometime. Once I get paid next month, let me buy you a swimsuit. Like a black one-piece. I hate bikinis, you know that? They cover up bad figures. Divide the body horizontally like that and you can't see the proportions properly. One-piece swimsuits show you a body just as it is.'

'I can't swim.' I kept my back turned. I wondered how Etsuko was going to act.

'You don't have to swim! Just wear it around the house or whatever.'

He grinned. I didn't answer. Etsuko could be a formidable opponent if you got on her wrong side. She definitely wasn't a plain old idiot.

'I can't get rid of the oil from the fish,' I said. 'I need some washing-up liquid.'

'It's fine, leave it. I'll do it later.'

I had my back to him. We said nothing for a while. When I turned around again, he was staring at my waist. He quickly picked up a dish towel for me.

'I got hard just now. Did you notice?' Not a flicker of embarrassment.

'How on earth could I have noticed?' I shooed him away.

'Better off not sleeping with you, right?'

I didn't answer. Maybe she'd slap me in the face. No, Etsuko was too proud. She'd never do something shabby like that, whether anyone else was watching or not. She might even act like she didn't care.

'You're too fond of destroying relationships,' I heard him say.

Maybe that's why she'd summoned me. To show me how unaffected she was.

'Once things seem to be going well, you smash it all up.'

'Right, I'm off.' I looked up.

'We've still got loads of time.'

'It's not like you're coming with me.'

'Come on, have a cigarette with me. To cap off the meal.'

I nodded, leaned against the bed and did as I was told. I thought about how to deal with Etsuko. It wasn't the first time I'd swiped a friend's lover. But I was less close to those previous friends. After it had happened, we'd act normally and gradually grow apart. That wouldn't play this time.

'She's done so much for me, been so kind. And look how I've gone and betrayed her.'

'You're a terrible woman,' he said, suppressing a grin.

'I wouldn't be surprised if I got myself murdered one time. Well, I suppose you can't really get murdered two times.'

'What a pathetic thing to say,' he jeered.

Suddenly I saw red and threw the nearest magazine at him. He ducked in time and it hit the wall, falling lamely to the floor.

'What the fuck? Come on, why are you like this all of a sudden?'

'I was holding it in till now. You're full of shit!'

That was a lie. But it started to seem like the truth once I'd said it. I flew to the door and tried to put my shoes on. One of the clasps wouldn't close.

'Where's this filthy mood come from?' He came closer and stood near me.

'Such a boring prick! I'd rather die.'

I managed to close the clasp while maintaining my tirade. I could barely catch my breath. Once I hit that stage, I get fully crazy with rage. Wonder why? Even I didn't know.

'I'm never coming to an ugly shithole like this again!'

Why did I say things like that?

'Hey, why are you so angry? I'm worried, you sound as if you hate me or something.'

'I do! I hate you!' It just slipped out.

'Because I won't come with you?'

'No! Because I can't look at your face a moment longer!'

I shot down the stairs at terrifying speed, slamming the door shut. Anger like this chases away any fear. I ran to meet Etsuko.

3

She's Got Us Talking

'Wait a sec, let me put some of this Tieguanyin tea on for us.'
Sabu got up.

I sank into the sofa and looked around the lounge of his
three-room flat. He had all sorts of odds and ends scattered
about. Green glass floats and fishing nets hanging from the
ceilings, and bigger versions on the floor. A rubber tree. Dried
flowers. Painted plates. A duck-shaped lamp. Andy Warhol
posters. Glass bottles in different shapes and colours. The clut-
ter and disorder felt good. His work desk was by the window.
He made rings and necklaces there.

'Where are the other two?' Sabu rented the place with two
guys who worked at gay bars, one aged thirty-five and the other
twenty-one.

'Madam's off doing some shopping.' Madam: that was the
older one.

'Laddie's seeing his kid.' The twenty-one-year-old was a
single father. The girl he'd been seeing gave birth and then

took off. With no other option, he had his parents take in the baby while he started working flat-out in gay bars. He was a sweet boy, but not the smartest out there.

'Your front door's weirdly clean.'

'That's because you came over when we were all out and decided to write up a huge announcement of your visit on that door in bloody marker pen. We had to scrub it off with scourers!'

Sabu took down some rice crackers from a shelf.

'It wasn't marker pen! It was eyeliner. You could've just used water. It comes off easily, no need for scourers.'

'Oh, my. You could have written that down for us, too.' He didn't seem bothered despite his words.

'I was with Ray. Poor kid had done it with me seven times that day, so he was totally spent. Kept having to sit down and rest under trees.' Ray was a friend of the comic-book artist I'd been to see before.

'That skinny lad?' Sabu asked.

'Yep. Looks aside, he's quite a clown. Bit weird seeing him trying to keep things smooth and suave while cracking jokes all the time.'

'Aren't you bored of these silly boys yet?'

'When we look at each other, we're all smiles,' I replied.

'Won't you start to see each other as friends? Then it'll get awkward.'

'Maybe.'

'Friends feel like siblings.' Sabu brought over the tea. 'If you do it with a pal it's like incest.'

'Exactly. That's why I do it right away with someone who's my type when I first meet them. Once you start hanging out and become friends, you can't do it anymore.' I nibbled on one of the rice crackers.

'I don't think it's like that for strait-laced folks. They spend half a year cultivating their love' – another of Sabu's phrases lifted from women's mags – 'then gradually, slowly, they start sleeping together. I can't believe it. I mean, once you really know each other, hanky-panky just gets awkward and embarrassing, doesn't it?'

'Yeah, and you end up joking about it. Once you've laughed too much together, you end up grinning at each other when it comes to crunch time. So, people who spend a long time "cultivating their love," the whole time they're aiming towards sex, right? Having sex is their ultimate end goal. How lecherous.' I reached to pick up a teacup.

'Careful, it's hot. I bought this tea down in Chinatown. Got some incense as well.'

The era's lingering hippy vibe, still hanging on to the tail end of its popularity.

'I don't understand these "platonic" hook-ups. I wouldn't be able to keep a straight face, I'd just burst out in the middle of it. You can't have sex while giggling all the time. The energy goes. You don't laugh at the height of it, do you?'

'Not usually, no.'

'And how can you fall in love with someone when you don't sleep together? I've never got the hang of unrequited love. If someone doesn't care about me, I immediately forget about them. I like men who make the effort.'

'Very womanly thing to say. Women are such realists.' Sabu had a different opinion to the comic-book artist.

'Exactly, and I've got more than my quota of womanly feelings.'

'Yeah, an excess.' Sabu grinned. He took some incense from under the table. The box had a Chinese-looking picture on the front. He also produced a big ashtray and lit four or five jasmine sticks at once. The smoke billowed up. Queens are so over the top about everything.

'I'm so possessive and jealous, I scare myself sometimes. I always want to be number one. Even if I don't like the guy very much, if ever he mentions another girl I go nuts. From barely caring to manically vying for his attention.'

'Nothing wrong with being extreme.' Only one of Sabu's eyes moved. His other was false. He'd lost that eye when it was hit by a stone that flew out of a nail-filing machine.

'You mean I'm deranged?'

'That's one way of putting it.' Sabu was calm.

'Wonder if being mad is a lifelong thing. Or maybe it wears off after a certain age.' I hugged in my knees.

'It's not something to be cured. Different story if you were ill, but . . .'

'Right. Because people call you crazy when you have an unusual approach to living in the world. If I were "cured" then I'd be a different person.'

'I don't totally get it,' Sabu said softly, 'but it seems that way.'

'When your world breaks, your self also breaks. But for me, the world's always been broken. It's all chaotic, out of my control. I'm sure that's why I try to sort and organise it so much. I want to have it all contained in the palm of my hand. Impossible, I know.'

'Are you always thinking through thorny stuff like this?' he asked.

'Pretty much.'

'So you're the cerebral type. You feel with your mind.'

'I feel with my body, too.'

'Which is strange. See, men use their minds when they sleep with women. It's not pleasurable if I only do things for my own benefit, they reason. So they need to please their partner as well. Whereas women usually follow their bodies, right? Some women are different, they feel things cerebrally. But what usually happens there is that they're suppressing their bodily selves. It's rare to have both sides active, like you have.'

'They come by turns now,' I said. 'It's like with a radio, I can't listen to both FM and AM signals at the same time. Imagine if I could listen to both. That's something to live in hope of. There we go, there's an aspiration.'

While we were talking, I wondered how Sabu could know so much about women. He can't have slept with many. He's a fag after all. Then I had a sudden realisation.

'I've got it! It's like I'm in drag.'

Sabu laughed. I laughed. He tugged on the hem of his shirt and scratched the back of his head, slightly apprehensively. Sabu's scalp had also been shorn, but since his hair was thicker than mine it just looked like a buzzcut.

'A drag queen is the bad parts of a woman distilled, right?'

Sabu tipped his head back in laughter at this. I went on.

'I didn't mean that as a dig at you. Being in drag is about deliberately emphasising your inner woman. Or if you're imitating a real woman, even then it's a case of cherry-picking her most extreme features. So it's still a distorted version. What I want to say is: I'm a female drag queen.'

Sabu smiled but looked uncomfortable. Teeth bared, I watched him squirm for a while.

He finally stood up, saying, 'I get it. As a woman, you're a one of a kind.'

'Exactly. There's no one else in the whole world like me.'

I felt shitty as soon as I'd said it. I knew I was wrong. I didn't know how to be right. I felt a sharp cooling in my chest. I had no self-confidence. Not like this.

Sabu sensed it and changed the subject.

'What happened with the lead guitar guy?'

'Got found out. I reckon someone told Etsuko.'

'It's likely. You two were hanging out around here in broad daylight. Stuck to each other like limpets.'

'He was just the right height,' I reasoned. 'I could cling to his chest.'

'You were at the florist's the other day, weren't you? I wonder why Yoyogi-Uehara has so many florists, high living standards perhaps. Anyway, you bought some yellow roses.'

'I gave them to him to take as a gift. He's close to his mum. He took those flowers back to his family's place in Kamakura.'

'He sounds gentler than he looks on TV.'

'He is. Doesn't talk much, either.'

'Your first time with a younger guy?'

'That's right. He's the same age as my younger brother. That put me off at first, made me think I shouldn't do it. It wasn't exactly guilt I felt, but something similar. Now, though, it doesn't bother me at all.'

'What a terrible moral compass. The sense that something's wrong doesn't usually go away once you get used to it.' He made sure to sound like he was telling me off.

'I've never had any morals, if I really think about it. In my teens I firmly believed I did, but it turns out I was just scared of other people who'd impose their morals on me. Once I'd realised that, it got horrific. Two or three times a year, I have these emotional blackouts. The worst ones last for several days. I avoid leaving the house when that happens. I feel I could kill someone, easy. I could do it and remain unaffected, like destroying a doll.'

'Must be tough, living with these mental quirks of yours. So what happened with the kid's girlfriend?' Sabu smiled as he played with a heavy ring he'd made.

'It's fine, we're friends again.' I felt dejected for some reason.

'You've got some weird friends.' He took another ring from a wooden box.

'Yeah, I wouldn't have let it go either, in her position. Makes you wonder.'

'If someone took him away, would you cry and scream all over the place?'

'Probably.'

'Spout out all the bad parts of a woman?'

'Yep.'

'Here, take this. Should be just the right size.'

Sabu handed me a silver ring. The design was of a mask and there were two clear stones in it.

'Thanks, are you sure?'

'It's nothing expensive. The stones are white zircon. Seeing you in your sorry state makes me want to give you something, that's all.'

'I'm just sad because it seems like I'm all bad.'

'Surely you must have a woman's good parts, too? I don't know.'

'What's that supposed to mean? Come on, I'm fishing for compliments.' I put the ring on my finger and held out my hand to Sabu insistently.

'Well, let's see. You're kind, for instance.' He suppressed a grin.

'Give me more!' I started sniggering.

'You're way more sensitive and intricate than you look.'

'Than I look? Well, fine, I'll take it. What else?' The ring made my hand look like an infant's.

'Oh – but wait, this is usually a male trait. Talking with you means using my brain. Most people are one way, but you're another. I have to bear that distinction in mind. And, let's see, you're good at looking cute?' Sabu was trying hard not to laugh.

'Oh, sod off!' I threw myself back onto the sofa and looked intently at the ring and my finger.

'Do you put a lot of work into it?'

'No, no.' I got up. 'It's something I've always had. It surprised me too, at eighteen. I didn't know why I was so good at attracting men, like it was some inborn talent. In my life I've only ever used what I was born with. Meaning that I've lived through the past twenty-three years without making the slightest effort. I've not acquired anything new. Anything technical I can do was just a matter of getting used to it. Without basic talent, you can't actually learn technical skills.'

'Come on, you do have talent, it's sexual. The sort of talent that crumbles if you try to use it professionally. Even temporarily: unless you genuinely feel love for who you're with, it won't work.'

'It's a shame though, I've only got a few years left to use this talent of mine.'

'Do you want to get married?' Sabu asked curiously.

'Yes, of course. Wouldn't it be lovely to rely on someone else. It would suit me. I'm the over-dependent type, not a drop of self-direction in my body. Even when I have feelings for someone, it's just a dependency, a deep need for affection. And I'll still want affection from every other man in the world as well.'

'Not satisfied with just a little spoonful?' teased Sabu, quoting Paul Butterfield. 'It's got to be a whole Pacific Ocean full of love?'

'Only three men have seriously proposed to me so far. Can you believe it?'

'That's average, out of context. But considering how many men you've slept with, it's a shockingly low number.'

'Etsuko insists every time we meet that she never wants to get married. But that's only because no one's ever proposed to her.' I was being nasty. About a friend who'd forgiven me, no less. Well, whatever. Those are two separate things.

'I bet she was nervous when you met up, right?'

'Oh, she's always like that.'

'Mm, I get it. I've seen her once before. With those looks, of course she'd end up dedicated to her job. No two ways about

43

it. I don't mean she was born with an unfortunate face, no –
it's her whole being, she's all stiff. Nothing fluffy or frivolous.
Always on her guard. Poor girl, I sort of pity her. If only she
were a little smarter, she'd find loads of ways to relax. Ways out
of herself, you know.'

'A week later she called me up and said that after some
thinking she'd realised he wasn't that important after all.'

'Sour grapes, eh.'

'She's a poor loser. She said: "It'd be a shame to lose a
friend as well." So I just accepted it right away, without
much thought. Felt like the natural thing to do, since she'd
forgiven me. Not thinking too deeply. No matter what
happens, I tend to accept it right away as the way things are
meant to be.'

'You let yourself go.'

Sabu ran his hand over his head slowly. He was quiet for a
while, then said the same thing again, this time fleshing it out.

'You let yourself go. You're fed up.'

If even someone like Sabu was saying this to me, it was a
sure sign that I had truly and thoroughly let myself go.

'I've been fed up forever.' I mean, no matter what happens to
me here, nothing would surprise me. Anything could feasibly
happen. Bad dreams don't follow logic. When I first became
aware of the world's cruelty, I felt a palpable despair at it. It was
created for me and it resembled a bad dream. I knew it was
futile to pray. There's been nothing for me to do since then but
give up, and remain utterly resigned.

Meanwhile my heart was pounding. In an incoherent,
inconsistent world, some exorbitant happiness could always

44

come along. I trembled at the premonition. I was in a world of man-made magic.

'So, Etsuko's fine with being deserted by her boyfriends?'

A strange way for Sabu to put it.

'Yeah. I suspect the reason she doesn't get attached to particular guys is because she has low sexual sensitivity.'

'She's frigid! Just say it,' Sabu laughed.

I grinned in response.

'So what's it like with this boy?' he asked.

'Just . . . ordinary.'

Foo held me so my head rested on his arm, and then he fell asleep. I began thinking about how I could sleep comfortably but without rebuffing this affection, and without cutting off the blood to his arm. I lifted my head very slightly, not enough for him to notice.

'Hard to sleep like this?' he whispered, eyes still closed.

I was surprised at how perceptive he was. Like a shy, alert animal.

I actually couldn't quite remember what it was like, even though we'd last seen each other only the week before.

'But he must be cruel in some way, being nineteen.'

'He is,' I said.

'When he came to my place that night,' Etsuko said, 'he told me straight away he had to go meet someone later. Come to think of it, he seemed weirdly restless too. But he's not very expressive, is he? I just assumed it was something to do with work. I gave him money for a taxi, and he used that to go to yours.'

'Isn't that incredible?' I laughed.

'Yeah. Definitely.' Etsuko laughed too. 'D'you think he's in love with you?'

'Probably not, he doesn't say he is.'

'He might be even if he doesn't say so,' she replied.

'No,' I said. 'Look. I never believe it unless they clearly say so. I don't want to play guessing games. I don't like making wrong assumptions. I try not to have any expectations. Lately I don't even trust what they actually do tell me. It's obscene to fall in love with me. Any man who does that is an idiot. But then when a guy won't fall for me, I hate it.'

'That makes sense to me, I'm also very suspicious. Still, I'm sure this one likes you. He's made a regular thing of coming to see you.'

'It's more like I'm a stopgap until he finds another proper girlfriend.' I really believed that. I didn't just say it for Etsuko's sake. Though I did decide not to tell her how Foo had spoken about their relationship. *There was this poster in a café we were at*, he'd said. *She was like, 'I've got the same poster. It looks way better at my place.' I mean, it's the same fucking poster no matter where you see it. So anyway, we went to hers. Then I couldn't just say ciao and leave . . .*

'Do you feel indebted to her, since she forgave you?'

'Not at all.' I made Sabu laugh with that.

'This is what I like about you. You're ungrateful. No matter what someone does for you, you treat it as your due. It's great.'

I wanted to say something but no words came. I started playing with some green glass beads. They made me think of Joel's eyes.

'Want something to eat?'

'I just ate with Etsuko in Harajuku,' I replied. 'We had some congee with prawns in it.'

'Let's have some tea then. I'll just boil the kettle again.' Sabu got up.

'Thanks.' I looked up at the ceiling. Whenever a waitress brought me my order in a café, I'd instinctively thank her. Once, a guy I briefly went out with snickered to see me do this. He said it was weird to thank the staff when we were paying good money for their service. Normally people didn't say thanks, according to him, they said: 'Sorry to bother you.' I felt like he was wrong. Surely it was even weirder to apologise. Still, he had some jaded authority, whereas I had no confidence. I'm meek and obedient deep down (honest!) so I stopped saying anything when my orders arrived. With friends I still ended up saying thanks. I didn't understand the rules of the world I was in. Meanwhile everyone else did, or so it seemed. That's why I was scared of other people. Sometimes.

'Are you closer now than before?' Sabu had lit the stove and turned back around to face me.

'We are. It doesn't feel like she's putting on an act. Even if she was, what good would it do?'

'True.' He stood in front of the stove and lit his cigarette. 'And what did you talk about?'

'She wanted to bitch about Mr Lead Guitar, so I obliged. Trivial stuff, though. She went on about how he gets completely

47

engrossed in sticking things up on the walls of the studio. "Mouth hanging open like a kid at nursery," she said, "happily snapping away with his scissors." Said she couldn't stand him being so childish.'

'I thought that was why she was into him?'

'Who knows. She also said Diana wasn't a patch on Green Glass.'

'She said it. Looking back, it's insane how popular Green Glass were in Yokohama. They were incredible. Even the obnoxiously discerning musos were into them.' Sabu was older than me. He was probably there to observe it himself.

'Then of course she starts heaping praise on Joel, the half-white guy.'

'That kid's not still alive, is he?' Sabu was surprised.

'I've heard nothing to the contrary.'

'Maybe it's just gossip. People around my patch were talking about it. A lot of gay boys like him too, you know. He's no soft touch. That famous Setsu Mode illustrator, you know who I mean, chasing after him in high heels and pink pants . . . Seems he's not into men, though. He's always swanning about with some fleshy girl on his arm. It was such a mystery to us. How could such a beautiful man be into women like that!'

Steam started coming out of the kettle.

'How do they say he died?'

'He got discharged from a mental hospital, did a load of drugs to celebrate, went out of a fire escape door on a snowy day and slipped in the shadows of the stairwell . . .'

'Very cinematic.'

'Yeah, like some new-wave ATG flick at that. It's pretty fishy.'

'Some girl, not Etsuko, told me Joel had syphilis. She said I'd catch it if I slept with him.' I stuck out my lower lip.

'Can see why she'd say that. It's good to have some scandal about you. Speaking of which, there's a girl called Yuka living nearby who says she used to date him. You could go and see her? She has a guy who lives with her too.'

Sabu poured hot water into the teapot.

'What kind of guy?' I was curious about Joel's successor.

'He's got long, thin lips. Like the cuff of a wide-sleeved dressing gown.'

'Blues lyrics are such shit.' Thus spoke Sleeve Man. 'Woke up in the morning, put on my boots, went for a walk. Ergo: Walking Blues. Then the one about the ocean running to the sea. Talk about stating the flippin' obvious.'

'There's one song about early morning being the start of the day too. It does sound cool because it's in English, but even so,' I said, my elbows propped up on their round table. It was the second time I'd been to visit.

The summer had grown thick outside. I sensed the seasons shifting when I was in some romance and I let my mind wander. Things were going calmly with Foo. I was neither excited nor fed up with him. I'd just decided that it was pointless hoping for any drama with that boy.

'They often start like that, don't they? "Woke up this mornin' . . ."'

This guy said that his band had split up before debuting. But what sort of band was it? Now he was living with this eighteen-year-old chick, and they walked to art school every morning holding hands.

'It's to signal the start of the story,' I offered.

'Exactly. Then when they open their eyes in the morning, usually a woman's left them. Then they get down and depressed. They sit on the bed and despair about life. Simple.'

I drank my apple tea. I'd been to Yokohama the previous week. I met with a girlfriend and we went for a walk. Foo came over that night and we shared a bottle of wine from the deli to celebrate his twentieth birthday. He was a Gemini.

'How about Nakanishi Rei, huh?' Sleeve Man said. 'He wrote a Honmoku-themed song for Green Glass. Lines like hate means hate, love means love. Yesterday is yesterday, tomorrow is tomorrow.'

'The blues is all about stating the obvious in your songs,' I told him.

'I wanted to give it a shot myself, but I just can't get as dark as those guys. I don't mean their own lives are dark. It's just the band's image. When I think of Green Glass, there's nothing light-hearted or easy-going. Everything's hammered out to the bitter end. Leaves me at a loss, to be honest. The guitar especially, it just won't give in. They had a sister band called Powerhouse, too, famous for how long their performances were.'

He started neatly picking out records from beside the speaker. First up was the B-side of *Blues Mind*, the third Green Glass LP. It started with an eleven-minute-and-ten-second rendition of 'Can't Keep from Crying Sometimes'. The original was by The Blues Project. We heard Landi's guitar squirming about, seamlessly linking one phrase to the next. I listened in admiration. So this is 'Chinese takeout' blues, I thought.

'Guys loved them. The audience at their shows would be mostly men. Landi was an idol for the wannabe guitarists. Those dudes would stand in the corner with folded arms, guitar case on floor, making it dead clear they weren't just there as common fans.'

'And listened with their eyes closed, I bet? Nitpicking the performance. Made their day if the guitarist slipped up. What dopes,' I said. 'If you're paying to be there at all, why not just enjoy it?'

'Guess it feeds their sense of superiority when they catch a mistake. Still, I think the most impressive one in this band is Joel. He's a real genius. Landi's more of a mental-effort kinda guy. The lead guitar only gets stuck in your head more because it plays the melody. Here's something: you know that music mag which does annual rankings voted for by readers? Two years in a row, 1970 and 1971, Joel was voted second-most popular. Obviously Sawada Kenji was number one. But to be number two when you're not a singer, that's pretty impressive.'

Sleeve Man seemed to respect Joel as an artist. Or maybe he felt strangely close to him through his current girlfriend's romantic history.

'His looks probably had something to do with it,' I said.

That same old summer began again this year. The endless summer, aimless dog days, burdened with a green-tinged fatigue.

'Well, sure. He is the archetypal ideal.'

Once summer started, all that joy and boredom made me abruptly lose weight. This year I lost four kilos. Foo asked me what happened. I hadn't the energy to get into it so I just told him: adults have their business. 'I prefer you this way,' he said.

Summer suits me because whatever will happen won't linger. Once the creaking light and humid air clears, it all seems like a lie. I pack it all up and stow it away on a high shelf. Take it down, open it up and it's always fresh as ever, thanks to a warped sense of time. No matter how many summers have passed since, summer from three years ago feels no further away than summer from two years ago, because nothing that happened in either has any relevance. There's no consistent, overarching storyline.

'In July the record label is putting out a double album called *The History of Green Glass*.'

The B-side was over. He started the A-side from the third track in.

'Lucille' began playing. It was the Everly Brothers arrangement, not Little Richard's version. An acoustic piano plinked tastefully in the background. It was a stylish, sensitive sound, conspicuously at odds with the player's pudgy physique. The blues needs a piano. No keyboard or organ will do.

'Someone asked me what a keyboard was the other day. I said it was a board with keys on it. Seems like the term hasn't caught on yet.'

'I don't think music is such an intimate part of most people's lives. Me, I decided once that I'd dedicate my life to rock music. But you don't get much in return for doing that, so I gave it up.'

Wasn't that perhaps more a question of his talent?

'What I don't understand,' I said, trying to cover up what I was thinking, 'is why proper professional studio musicians don't perform as well as these rough layabout kids from Honmoku. Take the Tigers' backing band, for instance. Their shows are totally dry.'

'Studio musicians don't do anything off-script, see. Besides, back then rock music had only just arrived in Japan. There weren't any experts.'

Yuka came back, carrying a paper bag.

'You're not playing that again? God, I'm sick of it.'

She sluggishly took off her shoes. She was plump-faced and short, but her chest and hips were developed enough.

'She can't not hate her ex's stuff,' Sleeve said.

'It's not on purpose!' She took some things out of the paper bag and put them in the fridge.

'What did you get?' Sleeve Man followed her into the kitchen to help.

Yuka turned to me. 'You hungry?'

'Not particularly,' I replied.

They placed a baguette, cream cheese and oranges on the table. Sleeve Man took particular care. I sat there and let myself be served.

'I reckon that kid's probably still alive.' Yuka's abrasive voice didn't suit her cherub face.

'Despite everyone saying he's gonna die soon, he's gonna die,' her man said softly.

'I met him the other day at the open-air stage in Hibiya, he seemed in pretty good spirits. Claimed he was off the drugs. I wonder how many times he's quit by now.' Yuka cut the bread on a fish-shaped chopping board. She went quiet, then suddenly said, 'Why does someone who looks so clean and beautiful have to get involved in such dirty things!'

'He's not that bad.' Sleeve Man took a slice of bread and spread some cream cheese on top.

'What the hell do you know?' she fired back.

'He'll spend the rest of his life clean,' he insisted. 'That era's already over.'

'Then he's just stubbornly surviving.' Yuka had her head bowed so I couldn't see her expression as she said it.

'Mind you, he doesn't look like the kind of guy who could live too long.' Sleeve Man seemed to be talking to himself. He turned to me to explain. 'The two of them first met when Joel collapsed on stage and got taken to a hospital run by Yuka's parents.'

'He'll just suddenly sneer randomly at nothing when he's walking down the street. Not laugh, but sneer. He sees things that aren't there,' she added.

'Who cares? He seems pretty unhappy,' I said casually, 'but hey, he's beautiful enough to make up for it.'

'He doesn't think of himself as tragic. His brain's been eaten away by all that glue.' She gave a bitter smile.

'The thing about unhappy people is that they tend to be grubby bastards, too.' I could think of several concrete examples of this. Myself for a start. Neither happy nor beautiful.

'So being unhappy is actually fine if you're beautiful? The opposite too, surely. No need to be beautiful if you're happy. That's less dramatic, though. Better to have some drama, so long as it's about someone else.' He maintained a strange coolness.

'A girl I know was in Ginza and saw Joel walking towards

54

her,' I said. 'It seemed like they'd just pass each other by, but then suddenly he reached out and grabbed her boobs. He'd gone a bit weird about sex, because the drugs he was on all the time meant he couldn't really do it.'

'I heard something similar from London Mary,' Yuka frowned.

'Oh, the Now Fashion Agency one? That's another girl who's famous for God knows what reason.'

Sleeve Man nodded. I continued:

'Apparently, when this girl went to see him in the dressing room, there were other people present but he undid his zipper and just laid everything out on display. Then he challenged the girl: "Mine's the biggest you've ever seen, right?" And when she didn't answer, "Okay, second biggest?" He kept at it. "Third? Fourth?" Even tried to get her to go into the toilets with him. But these stories get embellished so much, I don't know what to believe.'

It must be tough when you become a character in your own legend.

'Yes,' Sleeve nodded. 'You know what, I believe that man will always have an innocent, boyish heart, no matter what happens to him.'

'He's actually very endearing,' said Yuka, idly.

'And lovable,' her boyfriend added.

'I miss him.' Yuka suddenly sank into herself.

'But you've seen him again loads of times,' he consoled her softly.

'I still want to see him again, fifty more times.'

'Me too,' he said.

The night was approaching. The record had ended a while ago and the room was quiet. I finished eating my bread and picked up the cup of lukewarm apple tea. I took a sip then readied a cigarette. Sleeve Man lit the tip using a small gold lighter.

'You're Joel's type, you know.' Yuka seemed to have regained consciousness.

'What?'

'A good body like yours. He's into that. Hips that suit tight skirts. Hold on, let me give you his number.'

4

Honmoku Blues

I thought he'd have left long ago.

We'd arranged to meet at eleven o'clock by the Honmoku bus stop. Thanks to the mental retardation I retained from my childhood, I'd taken the Tokaido Line instead of the Toyoko Line and gone to Yokohama Station, and then the train was delayed. By the time I arrived it was past twelve-thirty.

Joel was standing there, serene. Looking like he'd walked straight out of the photos on that album sleeve. Slender and tall like a tree without leaves, not moving an inch.

I wondered whether he might be an idiot. I quickly parked my own blunder and looked down on him incredulously. What man waits nearly two hours for a woman whose face he's never seen? If it was in a café, perhaps – I suppose he'd have found ways to amuse himself, but even then he'd have to be a guy with nothing much going for him.

I approached him and he looked at me with those huge eyes. They might have been made of glass. Artificial, no human quality. The photos hadn't done him justice. He walked toward me wordlessly.

'Where are we going?' I had to break the silence.

'Fifteen minutes' walk away.' Joel didn't articulate clearly. His sentence tailed off, lacking confidence. His voice was low and unfriendly.

He turned around and added, 'I just rented a new place. Almost ten metres squared with a kitchen. Seventeen thousand yen a month.'

The Yokohama night had grown thick. I could see far along the linear neighbourhood streets but there was no one else around. We walked a while then turned onto a dirt path.

Something about him discouraged conversation. He stopped every now and then, turned around and waited for me to catch up. Our legs were such different lengths that his gait required a small jog from me.

His face was bare of emotion. His head was empty. Whatever once was there had been swept up and blown away by the wind one day. The man was like a vacant house with every door and window left wide open.

'I didn't expect your voice to be so deep,' he said suddenly.

'Yeah, people say it doesn't match my face.'

'I like a high-pitched, shrill voice. Child singers are great. Asada Miyo, Agnes Chan. Will they ever come to Yokohama? I'd definitely go to see them if they did. I'd wait outside the dressing room, hoping for an autograph, heart pounding.'

Just like his own fans used to do. I tried to laugh but it didn't come out. He was so blank and expressionless, it was frightening. Like an android. He stared at me (my body) with the clear eyes of someone mentally unhinged, or possibly just perverted.

'C-cup, thereabouts?' He kept speaking like this, in sudden spurts. But still there was nothing corresponding on his face. He was, decidedly, an idiot. An undeveloped animal brain with lightning reflexes.

'E-cup, actually. Eighty-eight centimetres on top, sixty-six centimetres underneath.'

'Wow,' Joel smiled slightly. 'How about that.'

Or has he been having me on the entire time, I wondered. He could keep a straight face because he wasn't taking me seriously.

'We are almost there.' He sounded demented.

We went up a gentle, winding flight of narrow stone steps. I walked slowly, watching my step. My eyesight wasn't great, so I often tripped. Joel lent me his hand. He was strong. He had musician's hands, big and long-fingered. I looked down, expecting him to pull me closer. (What a filthy-minded woman.) But he didn't embrace me.

'Why are you going red?' He moved very close. Serious now, apparently.

'What?' I tried to smile like a saucy temptress. Probably all that happened was that my face twitched. Didn't go so well.

He stopped and stood still, staring up at a second-floor apartment.

The lights were on inside. He turned around and touched his lips, then gestured at me to wait there a moment. He went up a metal staircase, stepping lightly to silence his footsteps. He peered through the kitchen window, then pondered for a while outside the door. He entered the flat quietly.

I thought he might live with a girlfriend. In that case I shouldn't have come. Still, my goal was modest. I wanted to see what this boy was really like. I didn't particularly want to *do* this or that. So, it shouldn't matter who was there.

Joel came back out after a time. 'Quietly,' he warned me, quietly. He went back in.

I mounted the stairs. With a heavy heart, for some reason.

'Go ahead.' Joel stood at the doorway. He was a dark silhouette with the light behind him. There were no curtains. A futon bed was still unfolded next to the window. One table, two chairs. An extremely high-quality sound system, approximately six hundred LPs. One guitar. Two electric bass guitars.

'This is my cousin,' he said, 'and this is his friend.'

It was pretty awkward. They'd clearly let themselves in uninvited while Joel was out. He wouldn't ask them to leave. Even if hints were dropped, they'd probably pretend not to understand. Then Joel would go all shy.

The cousin turned to everyone present, opened his arms wide and smiled grandly. He turned to me and asked heartily, 'How about some coffee?'

I nodded. No other option.

Joel lay down on the futon and rested his head on two pillows. Some music film was playing on the TV. It sounded pretty shoddy. I watched more closely and realised it was a Beatles performance.

'What about you, Joel?' Mr Cousin spoke very gently.

'Yes, please. Just a little milk.' He sounded like he was answering a scary mother. I sat on a chair. I couldn't calm down. I lay down on the tatami floor next to Joel and propped up my head with my hand.

'What?' I asked, turning as I realised he was saying something to me. But I couldn't make it out. His pronunciation was too unclear and his expression still completely blank.

There was a close-up on Paul McCartney's dumb-looking face on the TV. He was talking in Japanese. The dub was shitty. John Lennon and the rest of them were all so short. Were the Beatles a dwarf band?

Joel mumbled what seemed like the same words again. I couldn't understand.

'What did you say?'

He seemed embarrassed, but not frustrated. He persevered and spoke again.

'Use a pillow.'

Seriously, that was it?

He pointed to his side. We lay next to each other on the bed and kept on watching *A Hard Day's Night*. Seemed like it would go on for ever and ever, until the end of the world.

I drank the coffee and smoked a cigarette. I smoked recklessly.

'The songs don't match the scenes,' Joel said. 'What's "Can't Buy Me Love" got to do with this part?' He seemed relaxed.

'They're like the Monkees,' said the cousin.

'The Monkees are better,' said his mate.

I didn't care. I just wanted these two boys to leave.

The broadcast finally finished. Thank God, I thought. But there's more. Extra time to while away. The cousin put on a record.

'Don't play it too loud.' Joel was nervy. As if he intended to start afresh and live like an adult here. I made a show of looking at the records. He had most of the go-to rock stuff. I couldn't see Green Glass anywhere.

'Where are the Japanese bands?'

'Some stuff's still in storage, so in there probably.'

'What about Diana?'

'I like them.'

The conversation remained laconic.

Joel reached for his cigarettes on the table. I handed them to him. He thanked me. Some matches too. Thanked me again.

I was smoking incessantly again. I ended up coughing. Joel stared at my face. His eyelashes were incredible. Thick and dense, outlining his huge eyes and heavy lids. On the more dramatic end of Koji's false eyelashes range, 1,200 yen for a top and bottom set. He stroked my back.

'Let's sleep,' he said, indifferently.

The cousin and his mate brought out their own futon from the closet.

I stood with arms crossed and asked of no one in particular where to go. Joel made room by his side.

I shook my head.

'I don't like that side.'

Holding the pillow, I went over him, to the window side. I didn't want to be next to his cousin. What if he reached out in the night? No, it had to be Joel.

His mouth moved into a smile.

The lights went out.

I undid the hook on my blouse. It wasn't totally dark. There was some faint light from the street lamps outside. I wriggled out of my skirt. I put my clothes next to the pillow and settled in beside Joel. We didn't touch. I clasped my hands together above my chest. Everyone instantly pretended to be asleep.

I held my eyes shut for about fifteen minutes. My sense of time was haywire. One minute felt like a hundred years. I felt as if I'd smoked weed. I held on, motionless, and it felt like I'd wound up at the end of the world.

I checked Joel. He was facing straight up, his lips firmly closed. I leant on his shoulder. He grasped my hand and placed it on his chest.

I thought he might be asleep. Annoyed, I squeezed his hand. He moved my hand to his hip. He wanted me to touch him. But I couldn't. It's not that I'd become coy all of a sudden. I was in a state of total indecision. It was the first time I'd met a man like this.

Still trying to keep up the sleep charade, Joel reached up and pinched my nipple. He had no trouble finding it through my bra. I shivered. His face didn't move.

He held the back of my neck and drew me closer. He opened his eyes and turned to face me.

'Don't make a sound,' he whispered.

'Aren't they asleep?'

'They're just pretending.'

'But they seem asleep.'

'Right, *seem*.'

Another long period of time passed. Joel acted sound asleep but occasionally his hand, alone, would move. My head lit up each time. Like fireworks were going off.

He was wide open to me, so I placed my hand on his bare chest. The wispy tuft of chest hair surprised me so much that I held my breath. I'd never have expected something like that from his face alone. He seemed too like a doll.

'I'm awake now.' He looked up and smiled. He shifted his body and gazed at me. He was grinning, poised as if about to embrace me. I smiled back, limply. He touched my ear and whispered.

'If I didn't know *him* I'd be fine with going ahead. But I can't.' He looked over at one of the guys (apparently) snoozing. It felt strange to see Joel's eyes actually move. They resembled very realistic glass eyes with vast whites.

'Is he really your cousin?' They didn't match. Joel had a totally boyish physique, but he also had a sturdy frame and a solid chest. How tough it must have been, supporting that long neck (he must have a different way of moving his head to most people). It was as if he had a cousin who you'd expect to speak in a cheeky Osaka dialect; a man who couldn't be related by blood to the protagonist of a fairy tale.

'I locked the door before I went out. This was a surprise. He must've used a hairpin or something to get in.'

Of course this cousin had burglary skills!

He held me from above and asked solemnly: 'Can I come on your stomach?'

He trailed his fingers down to my hips and back up along my sides. He smiled slightly.

'This difference between here and here is driving me crazy.'

He lay on his back again, taking off the trousers he'd gone to bed in. (He must have been hot.) He didn't use underwear.

64

'Never?' I queried. Another surprise. I wasn't usually one to constantly marvel at every little thing.

'Not in summer. Too much hassle.'

Didn't that other twenty-three-year-old Yokohama man go commando too? Perhaps this is an issue requiring further investigation. He kicked his trousers aside.

He seemed pretty relaxed. He held me from above again. 'May I?'

I nodded. He entered me slowly. The size was yet another surprise. It hurt. My body wasn't excited yet at all, which didn't help. I mean, he was spooky. Expressionless. He didn't seem human in form or in character. It was like being held by a plastic doll with glass eyes. He was like a photograph. No eroticism, nothing so human.

I watched his face silently. So even people like this have sex, I thought. Partly in admiration. No matter how pretty a pretty boy is, he'll still grovel and beg to a woman. Please. Beg me more. You'll be beautiful no matter what you're doing.

'Do you like that?'

Joel brought his face closer. I looked at his dark eyebrows. Brown like his hair, neat diagonal lines.

'Do you like it?'

Did I like it? Search me. He had good instinct and he knew it. That's quite a skill. But he was so lackadaisical about it.

'Like it?'

He kept asking the same question. As if he was taking care and being gentle. Not to scare me. Well, I was already scared. From the moment I'd seen his looks. His basic concern seemed only to be whether I was feeling something or not. In this case, that was my responsibility.

'Hey, you like it?'

I nodded. I got the sense that I seemed to like it. (In terms of sexual pleasure, however, it was way off.)

The guy next to us turned over in his sleep. It was too slow to be real. Joel looked over at him. He lifted his head and grinned at us. Joel's eyebrows shot up and his mad eyes turned an odd colour.

'Got an audience, huh.' Joel laughed and buried his face in my neck. I closed my eyes tight shut. My brain was excited. I felt it with my mind. My body didn't move. I knew the smoothness of his skin. He was almost too well put together. A slender but pliable man's body. I let out a long breath.

'Did you come?' He sounded concerned. I wanted to wrap things up, so I nodded. He moved off me and rolled to the side.

'Shall we go somewhere else?' I felt composed. What else could we do. Someone was watching us right there, plus Joel didn't seem to be enjoying himself one bit.

'That's what I was thinking.' He looked up and pinched his chin. 'You got any cash?'

'Just a thousand yen.'

'That's plenty!' He laughed. 'I've got five hundred. No chance of a hotel.'

He turned back around. He was brimming with an innocence that didn't fit with his face. His lips were thick and soft. Both corners of his mouth hung down in invitation.

'Kiss me.'

He did. His puffy lips moved away. He was like a small, non-lechy version of Mick Jagger. Had his neck been one

centimetre longer, he would've looked creepy and grotesque.
As it was, he already looked like some neck-stretching demon.
With those proportions he could even have got into a freak
show. It wouldn't be so out-there to call it a deformity. He'd
walked straight out of a fashion designer's sketchbook or a
comic book about pretty princes.

'Wait till morning.' There was no fire in his voice. He gripped
my fingers. 'They'll leave. Then we can do it.'

I was reassured by the transparent simplicity of a twenty-
four-year-old. 'I heard you quit the drugs?'

'Yeah. I'm not doing them anymore. I put some weight on.
I've been at the pool all the time this summer. I even got a tan.'

He held my neck, then slipped into sleep in the same
position.

A finger sheathed in a piece of metal pipe glides along the
strings. Slide guitar. Or bottleneck, some call it – players used
to cut off the top of a liquor bottle and stick that on their finger.

The Yokohama Blues. (Does such a thing exist?) There
you can hear the blues from across the ocean. (It could be
anywhere, though.)

Court a quiet sadness. Drop those Es and Bs a half-tone.
Make me sick with your love. Make full use of your polished
operations and techniques. As long as we get there without
becoming serious. It doesn't matter if it's not how we really
feel. Our real feelings are exhausting. Let's put them off until
later.

I put my fingers on Joel's skin and closed my eyes. His solid
arm held my head to his neck. His old singing voice came back
to me faintly. Pronunciation flat and negligent. Echo effect

switched on. He's singing alone, far away. The levels soar and dip on repeat. Feels like tripping. Maybe I'll never cry again.

It was morning, but the cousin and his friend still hadn't left. It suited them to play dumb.

Joel was pretending to be asleep. Covers drawn up to his chin, not moving an inch. The brownish contour of his body under the covers made him look like a mummy. Belatedly embarrassed. Having been watched.

I was totally fine. Times like that made me feel like a woman. It's a woman's special skill, being shameless, and occasions like this are when it's on full display. I don't get bothered. Readily surrender myself. Easiest is best.

The cousin and companion decided to listen to Paul McCartney and Wings.

Joel sprang up suddenly. He clung to the window. He stared at the street below. He was still watching solemnly even after the record ended. The sound cut off. The arm on the record player returned to its place. A small, sharp sound, then the machine turned off. He swivelled.

'Hey, has the garbage truck been yet?'

That threw me for a loop. I thought his long observation would beget a better question.

'I've got to take it out for them to collect today. They won't come again till the day after tomorrow!' It seemed like the rubbish was the only thing Joel could think about. 'I don't like to leave food waste sitting there in summer!' Guess he didn't have the habit of holding two thoughts in his head at once. 'I always make sure I properly sort the trash, you know!'

'Let's eat something,' the cousin suggested. 'I'll go and order in. It's not far. What do you want?' There was no phone in the apartment. The friend said he wanted tempura and soba noodles. The cousin looked at me and Joel.

'Simpler's better,' I said. 'Like toast or something.'

'Agreed. I'll make some.' Joel went to the kitchen. He peered inside the paper bag he'd been carrying the night before at the bus stop. The cousin went out and came straight back. Ten minutes later the food arrived.

Joel made coffee. I was sat by the window. He asked whether I took milk, whether I took sugar. I took my cup of coffee into the kitchen. I watched Joel's back as he made the toast. He turned around and smiled slightly.

'Show me your nipples. It was too dark to really get them last night.' He pressed me to the wall. 'I like seeing them.'

I undid the hook on my blouse and reached into my bra. He looked, attentively. His eyes had turned yellow and brown in the morning light.

'Nice fresh colour, aren't they?'

We could hear the sound of noodles being slurped. Those two were listening in, no doubt about it. Didn't stop Joel from giving his review of my appearance. 'Your body's nice and tightly put together, considering its size.' What a jerk. But why do men always praise women's bodies? They all do it, almost like they'd come to some agreement about it. They never, ever skip the compliments.

Joel, satisfied with the colour of my nipples, brought a plate of toast and ham back into the main room. I followed him. He was silent for a while then started speaking, seemingly to himself. This time it wasn't about the trash collection. 'I've got to meet some new bandmates today.' I wondered where in his head the waste issue had moved to.

Since leaving Green Glass, Joel had been in a cycle of joining and leaving one band after another. He was never the frontman, but always led around by the others. He wasn't particularly bothered or driven by anything. He just plodded along with music somehow.

'I was in Kyoto recently. At Mama Ringo.' An infamous live music club. The Group Sounds scene had had its day and the survivors were flowing out west, to Kansai. 'I've got to go again. That's why I broke up with the girl I was living with. Last month.' He laughed. 'I've not had many women come over lately.' He seemed to be thinking about something. Whatever was inside his head was surely so atypical that I couldn't even guess at it. 'What time is it?' he asked.

'Almost two o'clock,' the cousin replied.

'Really.' Joel stretched his neck and stared into space. He seemed to make up his mind, then he put on a T-shirt. 'I'll walk you to the station.' I was pretty sure he was just talking to me, but of course the cousin and his friend came too. By now it'd become beyond inconsiderate.

We walked along some hedges. A white butterfly flew about. Joel pretended to catch and let it go. He turned to me, grinned and said, 'See what I did just now? Just showing that butterfly who's boss.' What a jerk. It was a girlish thing to think, but I thought it all the same.

5

Three in the Morning

'Don't you find you get tired of men more quickly now?'

'Umm . . .' I gave Etsuko some vague response. There's depth in not decisively agreeing.

Three in the morning.

Joel had written some lyrics.

Monday morning, three o'clock.

He sang them on their second album.

Someone told me, three o'clock.

That's it. Psychedelic guitar, falsetto chorus. Very gaudy, no substance.

Sadly, it wasn't a Monday. It was past midnight, already Sunday, and Diana's lead guitarist hadn't called for three weeks. Our situation had ended along with the summer. I don't like holding out, so when Etsuko asked me to go for a drink I said yes.

'I feel like I'm through with men,' she announced happily. Etsuko was so upbeat that I felt a bit lonely seeing her. We were at a rock café in Shimokitazawa. Three long-haired guys were settled at an adjacent table. Long hair didn't do it for me.

'Depends on what they're like,' I said. 'If I picked up one of that lot off the street? A week or two and that would be it.' I was feeling dispirited.

'It's more like three days for me!'

A bunch of cosmos flowers sat in the middle of the table. Pink and white, mostly pink.

'. . . Or barely a few hours, nowadays!'

Etsuko took a sip of her whisky for greater emphasis. How lonely, I thought, if that's really how she feels. I couldn't imagine a life without falling in love.

'What's it like for you?' She wasn't holding back. Such a pointed question from her caught me off guard, shook me out of the Creedence Clearwater Revival track I'd been lost in for a moment.

'The longer I've known a guy,' I began, 'the more attached and yet more bored I get, both at once. So I *do* get tired of them. But then I also like them a lot more than when I first met them.'

I spoke more softly than Etsuko. My speech got thorny in conversation with men, though.

'Are you talking about Foo?' She looked perplexed. She'd totally given up, and she wanted me to do the same.

'Yeah. I'm sure he's found another woman.'

'Well, you know. His band's peaking now, they might even be past their prime. He can probably take his pick of people to sleep with.'

'Right. I never call him. We didn't make any promises or anything. It's just me, waiting for him to call.'

Etsuko's eyes widened at this.

'Sounds awfully nice and convenient. For him, that is.'

'Yeah,' I agreed.

'Very calm about it, aren't you? I don't get that about you. It's like no matter what happens, you're just coolly watching, not a care in the world. You're so young.'

'I'm not young at all. For me, anything goes. No matter how outrageous. I've always been like this, even as a kid. It's a severe form of resignation.'

'Huh.' Etsuko was unsettled. 'So, Joel, do you like him?'

'I think so. My period started after I met up with him and it hasn't stopped. I've been going to a clinic a minute's walk away every day. I'm getting hormone injections. They say my uterus is bleeding abnormally.'

'Oh, no.' Etsuko leaned closer to my ear to say, 'Actually, the same thing's happened to me.' She moved away again. 'I heard it's from nerves. I guess we're both emotionally unstable.'

'Are you unstable?' I tried the direct route.

'I suppose so. I'm pleased, though. I finally managed to get in touch with Yoko Ono. She accepted my request to interview her. I'll be the first Japanese woman to do it! I get to go and meet her in New York.'

She shivered slightly. I wondered if it was excitement, like a soldier before battle. I could probably never feel as passionate about work as Etsuko did. Not even once I'd grown old and lost my charm. What would I do as an old woman?

'I was so happy.' She did seem excited.

'Do a good job,' I said lifelessly.

'You always seem so weary.'

'My body's not very robust. If I were stronger I'd see things differently. People who get these little fevers all the time, like me, live in a different world to those who don't.'

'I think you live more in the mind.'

'I reckon your mind gets influenced loads by the physical body you're born with. Our feelings or whatever are easily moved by material reality. I mean, think about it. Women care more about a stranger at hand than a faraway lover.' I was really flagging, maybe because I was still bleeding. My glass of whisky and water felt so heavy. Must eat more protein, I thought.

'But it's not just women who are like that, is it?'

'I don't know about men. And about women, all I know is my own case. I still think it's silly to say falling in love is only about the emotional stuff. They say a woman's afflictions run deep, don't they? Her mind can decide to hate a person, but her body won't stand for it. She knows she shouldn't have feelings for her lovers, but still she misses them and ends up in their arms. Acting guilty about it is her way of satisfying both pride and desire at the same time. It's very crafty.' The cosmos flowers drooped. I was tired too.

'But you don't suffer from any affliction or foible like that, do you?' Etsuko seemed to expect me to be more like a man.

'Nope. Because I don't hold myself back. I also don't care about pride, or appearances.'

'I basically subsist off pride,' Etsuko murmured indifferently.

'Pride's abstract, right? Something that might exist. I don't need to rely on stuff like that, I find confidence in other things.'

Maybe I shouldn't have said that. I was tired, I couldn't control myself.

'Well, everyone has different priorities,' I added.

Etsuko shook her head slowly. 'Exactly. You're right. Maybe if I had a body like yours,' she said, 'I wouldn't need to cling onto my pride like I do.'

I was about to disagree but decided against it. She'd put into words a thought I'd had myself. Only vaguely, but still.

'Come to think of it,' she went on, 'it's a pretty starry-eyed idea to like your own body. People who assume they're psychological types tend to overestimate the strength of their mind and emotions too. All they need do is run into someone wicked' – she paused to glance at me and smile – 'and then they crumble.'

'I'm kind, right?' I said.

'Yes, to any and all.' She smiled again.

'Anyone I'm with, male or female. My main principle is to let everything pass.'

'Special skill of the cold-hearted.'

'Exactly. Warm-hearted people tend to be nicer to those they're close to, and pretty awful to anyone they're not. I can't stand it. I don't allow myself to be fonder of someone just because of some connection we happen to share.'

'Most women do exactly that. Fall for someone because that person's been kind to them. But you, even if a guy's nice to you, you'll hate him if he does bad things to other people.'

'Because I'm watching from a slight distance. I fall for people like they're characters in a TV show. It's just like watching a film. I can watch three different films and enjoy them all in three different ways. That's how I can be in love with several people at once.'

75

'You're terrible.'

'Absolutely,' I agreed.

I could only get my body drunk with alcohol. My brain stayed stubbornly lucid. I was too used to it, to booze and drugs.

'You're just cold-hearted, aren't you?' She seemed pleased about this for some reason.

'Maybe I am. I mean, the reason I'll let anything pass is so as not to interfere in anyone else's life. I never tell people what they should do. I'm not kind in *that* way. If I changed them, I wouldn't be able to see their natural selves anymore. "Do everything just the way you want to." It's basically the same as saying, "Do whatever you like, it's none of my business".'

As I spoke I started to scare even myself. Was it really okay to carry on like this? I could be wrong, I wasn't sure. Etsuko's glass was empty. She put in some fresh ice and whisky. Topped it up with some mineral water, then reached for my own glass. I shook my head.

She took a sip of her new drink. 'And you're this way even with me?' She gently brought the conversation home.

'Yes.'

'But you know, even if you didn't intend to, you've really influenced me. You're pretty fucking weird. Intense and strong, but you don't force your ideas on people. You accept what someone does and thinks exactly as they do it, unfiltered.'

'Like a mirror?'

'Which means I learn all sorts about myself when I spend time with you. And I'm not saying there's nothing to you, that you're a blank slate, not at all.'

'I wouldn't care if I was.' I wasn't being moody. I'd be totally fine with it if there really was nothing to me. It was unnerving. Sometimes I even wished I were more flat and frictionless.

'It's reassuring being with you. I feel accepted as I am.'

'I wonder if Foo feels that way too,' I smiled wickedly. 'It's not good to let a man feel too safe.'

'They need a little push and pull sometimes, eh?'

One of the three long-hairs had been making eyes at us for about twenty minutes. I thought so, anyway. My eyesight wasn't good enough to tell.

'Hey, what's that guy look like?' I craned my neck slightly.

'Lower ranks, I'd say. Going by your standards.'

'No good?'

'None. Especially now you've nabbed the ultimate in pretty boys yourself.'

'Joel's gone off to Kyoto.'

I avoided looking at the long-haired crew as much as possible. I was tired and couldn't be bothered.

'Then do something about it, girl.'

'Give me a break.'

'I've heard he's got a memory like a sieve,' she teased.

'No difference between a girl he slept with once and a curry he ate sometime, right? For him at least.'

'Well, he's in high demand. I heard the blonde go-go dancer at Astro in Motomachi is crazy about him too.'

'I've been phoning Mama Ringo,' I said.

'You should just go to Kyoto.'

'Someone as gorgeous as him would never fall for me properly.'

That's what I genuinely believed. Etsuko searched for some words to comfort me, but deep down she agreed. 'Who knows,' she murmured.

I opened my bag and took out my purse. 'Let's go.'

'I'll do a great interview. Just you wait!'

She still seemed keen. So long as she's lively, I thought.

I got home after five o'clock. The phone rang immediately.

'I've been calling you over and over.' Mr Lead Guitar sounded like he'd been about to give up.

'I was with Etsuko. She's going to America.' I reached out to turn on the bedside light.

'I booked a hotel room in Shinjuku. I've been waiting for you for three hours.' (Should've called another girl then.) 'No other girl will do. It has to be you.'

I inspected the collection of candles next to the phone, all different shapes and colours. An art director had bought them for me the week before. The shop was in Harajuku and sold rattan baskets and trinkets made from feathers. I met up with that guy roughly once every three months. He always bought me gifts.

'Could you come now? Even though I might be a bit tired,' he said.

'I'll come.'

He told me how to get there. I went out onto the main road and waited for a taxi.

I took a small green compact out of my pocket and lightly dabbed the tip of my nose. It was September already. There were just thick layers of fatigue left now. Next up was my hated

October. I couldn't stand its damp, calm composure. The bill-boards advertising cosmetics around town were already firmly ensconced in their autumn aesthetic. Then would arrive the dark, stagnant days of November, which I hated even more. I grew weak-hearted in winter. I'd just be waiting for March to come. I met no good men in the cold.

I opened the door and he hugged me.

'I've been waiting all this time.'

I sensed the end of romance in his husky voice.

The lights weren't on. The heavy curtains were closed. Still, the whitish, cool light of morning slipped through the gaps and soaked the room.

'I think I'll have a wash.'

'Me too.'

There wasn't much hot water. I got out of the bath straight away and rubbed myself vigorously with a towel. Next, he took a shower. We'd never bathed together. My sexual involvement with this boy was always very plain and straightforward.

I got into bed feeling leaden. His cool, slightly damp body held me from the side.

'I slept with this foreign eighteen-year-old the other day.' Foo looked up as he spoke. 'She smelled bad, had pretty intense BO. I couldn't get in the mood at all. Didn't even get hard. I find a girl has to be at least half Japanese for me to get there.' He turned back to face me. 'We didn't do anything all night. Seriously.'

'Okay.'

'Do you believe me?'

'Yes.'

I believe people with ease. That's why I don't react too much even if I find out I've been fooled. Whatever goes down, I don't care. I easily fall for people, I easily tire of them.

'Why do you take everything I say so seriously?'

'What's the point in doubting you?'

'I don't lie to you. But you're totally different to other girls.'

'What are other girls like, then?'

'They try to get me to swear all these oaths. Don't see anyone else, please, tell me you love me, that kind of stuff. But not you, not at all. You don't force anything.'

I felt remote from the figure of this boy talking at my side. There'd been a sense of isolation between me and him from the start, and I left it alone. I never tried to close that gap. If he'd wanted me to, maybe I'd have done it. Feeling distant was both lonely and comfortable.

'Should I hassle you more, then?'

I placed a finger on his neck. The window was behind him. It was too dark to read his expression. Not that he was the sort to wear his emotions on his sleeve. He could probably see my face clearly.

'No.'

He put his hands on either side of my waist.

'I like you just like this.' His simplicity was sweet.

I could probably adjust to whatever sort of person they were. I'm just not a protagonist. I live very noncommittally, I'm like water. I flow easily into any vessel and take its shape.

'You don't have the slightest BO, either.'

He stroked the hair at the nape of my neck. It'd grown pretty long. I looked at him silently. I became rather taciturn when I was with him.

'You've got light, smooth skin. A thin waist.'

'That's enough?'

'Yes,' he nodded. 'I'm satisfied.'

I mean, there wasn't anything I needed to tell him about. There wasn't anything for me to do apart from be held, quietly.

'Wanna smoke?' I moved. Realised I'd got sick of this kid.

'Sure.'

I lit a cigarette and handed it to him.

Yep, probably. Sick of him. After all, I'd never once thought about when we would split up. If a guy makes me think about that a lot, it means I'm still attached to him. To think that I missed this one when we couldn't see each other. And now that we'd met up, I felt nothing.

'Yaguchi's really starting to get on my nerves. Our frontman. Everyone's saying it.' I'd been hearing this complaint since around our third date.

'He's always too pushy about everything. I'm done with that band.'

This harshness coming from such a quiet boy. His voice slipped past and over my head. I replied on autopilot. Maybe it was here, I thought. My infamous feeling of a void that sucked me in a handful of times a year. My terrifying disease.

But no, it wasn't that. Joel's wide eyes were there watching me, their whites against the darkness, irises a clear green, lashes thick and brown.

'Then, like, you know the other guitarist, he was beating them with a stick, and my job was kicking their heads in.' He was now talking about a fight he got into in Roppongi.

'When I was at school I got hit in the eye, in another fight. Fucked up my sight in this eye.'

'Must have blinded you, surely?' I was hardly listening. I managed to respond, at least.

'Too right. I couldn't see for a while.'

This was an extremely introverted kid, and yet with me he was so talkative.

'You're always gentle with me.' Compared with other men. Almost too gentle.

'Well, you're a girl.' He kissed the nape of my neck. 'And I'm really into you.'

'Am I the best?' I asked.

'The best.'

The best, the worst. Those were his only value judgements. He fell asleep. I sighed meaninglessly.

6

Nights in White Satin

I was walking through Aoyama, held in Landi's arms. We couldn't have been more tightly pinned together. His arms were strong. He was deft. Even though we were glued to each other it wasn't at all difficult to walk.

I began to let my awareness slip. I felt I was being protected and it was comforting. I felt like I was in a dream.

Landi was Chinese. He turned his head and spoke to me. His slanted black eyes had clearly defined eyelids. They looked straight at me. I'd never met such a straight gaze before. A cocky bastard, I thought. But surely he'd never look at a man like this. No chance. This was his technique for picking up girls. It was a most refined skill. I'd been fully ensnared and by then was already getting light-headed.

'You. Stone.'

Most of what Landi said made little sense. But so what? His penetrating, metallic voice and clear-cut pronunciation alone had a powerful enough effect.

'Rolling Stones?' I tried, but it didn't matter. Just being held by him wiped my mind. His whispers in my ear were overwhelming. I went blank, couldn't think a thing. The night was thick and deep. So thick and deep there was no room for regret. (Even I had my regrets sometimes.)

'Yours. Let's go.'

Landi relaxed his grip. Hailed a taxi. Held my hand in the car.

I had been to see his band at a college festival. He was fatter than when he was in Green Glass. His guitar was almost perched on top of his pot belly. 'Lucille' didn't sound as good as it used to. I still thought he was fantastic. I couldn't help it. He was so lascivious, he oozed sex. And I'd thought I only liked skinny boys. I made my way to the dressing room when they were done. A dozen other girls were standing by the entrance. I was optimistic. He'd choose me. I looked the most garish and vulgar.

The floral pink curtains were fully drawn. The lights were off. Whenever I expected to get home late, I always left them on. I thought I'd be back early this time. I didn't foresee the developments with Landi. The last time I'd tidied up was the day before. A half-made bead necklace, materials and tools were scattered across my almost psychopathically large table.

'Two thousand cockroaches,' Landi said. The quality of this man's voice alone made an impact, no matter what he said. It could be utterly banal, didn't matter. 'It's the blues.'

He sat on his chair at a jaunty angle. I was blushing too much. I couldn't calm my heartbeat. I sat on the bed. I found it hard to breathe in this thick air Landi brought with him. I had to say or do something. I couldn't calm down. I stood up. I crossed the room, heading for the kitchen. I passed by him and suddenly he grabbed me.

'Just . . .' I struggled weakly against his grip. 'Putting the kettle on!' I felt faint.

'No need.' His grip tightened. He breathed down my neck. His breath smelled fleshy. That was all it took to transfix my body. He pulled me to the bed. I couldn't resist. Not that I wanted to. He got on top of me and peeled my clothes off. Lips to my neck and hair all the while. Very swift. Almost too good at it.

A sweet numbness spread in waves from the rear of my head. It felt like being in love. To lose myself like this with someone I'd only just met. I was tasting a playboy's wiles. Once he'd removed all my clothes, he pulled away for a moment. Stared as though carrying out an inspection.

'Great body. What a waste.'

What was being wasted?

He enveloped me from above. Held my breast, sucked my nipple. I couldn't see anything. It was too much. I shook my head from side to side. I may have made some noises.

He entered me, shivered slightly. Then said in a low voice: 'Filthy, aren't you?'

I turned away. I didn't want him to see the look on my face.

'Just dripping wet.'

He pushed harder. He was in all the way. I let out a stifled shriek. He moved violently. It seemed like he wanted to get it over with quickly.

'███. Try saying it.'

He told me to say a certain word, gently at first. No, I was so embarrassed I could die.

'Say it! ████!'

'No,' shaking my head. He had me under his thumb. This was probably the first time I'd been so utterly at the mercy of a man. It was quite something.

'Say it!'

'No.' I kept shaking my head. I'd completely fallen for his ploy. That word had worked so keenly on me. He carried on with the same forcefulness. His black eyes were no doubt open, watching. Watching and enjoying it. He watched everything. I couldn't hope to do anything close to the act of watching. Then suddenly, the feeling came.

'I'm coming,' I said. I was surprised. It was never like this the first time. 'I'm coming,' I said again. It was deeper than usual, undeniably deep. I stretched out my arms around him, ran my hands up his back.

'It's okay,' he said.

My hands wanted to hold him more, rubbing his back. I couldn't help myself.

'Come, it's okay.' He spoke softly all of a sudden. He was trying, for me. I never knew that being pinned down by a large body would feel so good. 'Come,' he said. He quickened.

My eyes were closed, I saw pitch black. I fell. I clung to him.

'You came?' His voice sounded far away. I nodded. I opened my eyes a crack. 'Again?' His face was so close, his black eyes. 'Feel it more,' he said. I was out of my mind. 'Even better,' he whispered. 'Quick!'

He was almost there too. He couldn't speak. His movements became even more frenzied. He pulled away. I felt him luke-warm, spilling onto my stomach. Hold me tighter. A pulse beating between us. Erupting again, again. He was still for a while.

Landi got up. He took some tissue paper and wiped my stomach. He let out a long breath and sat on the bed.

'You made me do it. I'm tired.' He sounded annoyed.

That set me off. But I was used to my own temper, and I hid my anger very skilfully. I don't think it showed.

'My wife's pregnant with our second kid. This is the first time I've cheated. I never planned this.'

Once you've done it, you can say anything.

'Before I got married I saw women as containers for discharge. She was a model. But she also runs the home and the restaurant well. I didn't know a woman could be like that. So I never gave in to any other woman who tempted me.'

Do what you want.

'Our signs are both Cancer. So family is important to us.'

Musicians are strangely fond of things like astrology. Their business is with the carnal senses, so maybe they're drawn to ideas that contradict them. I thought about telling him I was the same sign, but I held my tongue. I'd turned twenty-four in July. Landi was about two years older.

'I've got your perfume on me. I'll have to go to the sauna.' He was upset. He had no spare capacity to care about the woman in front of him. 'I've got to be back in Yokohama by midnight. I promised.'

He started putting his clothes on. I stayed there, naked, and watched him.

'I'm a fat bastard, but I've still got it.' He fastened his belt.

Yes, you have. You're an erotic man. Women throw themselves at you. Must be tough ploughing through them all. A man who recognises that in himself, *that's* a man who's truly still got it. I admired him. At the same time, I let out just a little of my anger from before. In a perfectly childlike voice, with a perfectly childlike look on my face, I cocked my head to one side and said, 'Is it 'cause you eat Chinese food?' Was it that fattening?

'Actually, I usually have toast for breakfast.' He hadn't noticed my nastiness. I was secretly glad. But I didn't let it show. He was about to leave. That's when he finally noticed my mood. He came back to the bed.

'It felt good with you,' he said.

I was curled up, knees to chest. He hugged my whole body from above. Very tenderly. I knew it was an act, but I bought it.

'I do want to see you again.' It almost sounded as if he was baring his true feelings. 'But I decided not to cheat. I've never done that before.' Now it was like he was talking to a pet or a child. 'We meet again and it'll keep happening. I can't do that to my wife, I don't want to be unfaithful.' You've already done it, pal. I saw how you lost yourself. 'So I'm sorry, love, but this can't go any further.'

He looked at me. How useful it must be to have his almond-shaped eyes. No one could suspect him of lying, with that gaze. All he had to do was gaze. Any anger inside me crumbled away.

And that's how it is. I forgive so easily, always. See, there's nothing certain in my life. It's all just like a dream.

'Got it.' I murmured this docile response. He hugged me, then left. I stayed unmoving on the bed, like a doll left in the trash.

7

Gimme Little Sign

'Scandalous,' said the blues singer.

'What is?' I leant against the sofa in my BIGI suit.

'Your musician sprees of late.'

Ai stood by the window in a long black stage dress. She hooked her fingers into a slit in the green shutters and peered outside. It was past midnight in Roppongi. But the only view was of the wall of the building opposite.

'Is it really such a small world?' I tried a startled tone of voice, shook my head, all that.

'You betcha.' She turned around slowly. Her hair hung low and touched her face. 'Everyone's bored, you see.'

'How awful.' I didn't really think it was so bad, but I said it all the same. 'So once a few of you get together you just end up gossiping? Who's bedding who, that stuff.'

'Well, musicians don't have the broadest of interests. Especially the ones who entered the business in their teens. They never got the chance to learn any social skills. Didn't need any, their manager would handle it for them.'

'We're not smart, us lot, we don't get the complicated stuff, so . . .' I jutted my chin out and did my best inane-rock-musician impression.

'They do the same thing day in, day out. It's even simpler than it looks from the outside. Main topics are music and sex.'

'Yeah, I know. But I wonder how you heard about it. Aren't you more on the jazz side? If you had to say. Or am I wrong.'

'No, I'm pretty into rhythm and blues too.'

Ai sat in the chair opposite. She gripped the velvet armrests. Even when we met at home like this, she always posed for some hidden camera.

'I was relieved to hear it, though. Glad you're getting out there and doing your thing. It's good. When you stop getting laid, that's when it's all over.' Ai spoke lazily, her voice heavy and dry.

I said nothing. Love felt like an endless, futile toil to me.

'I did a gig with Green Glass about four years ago. That's the only time I did a Group Sounds thing. Hard to believe, isn't it?'

'You'd sing "Stand by Me"? Not just "Gin House Blues"?'

I pictured the stage. Truly bizarre. Here was this left-field singer coming out all sultry and dark. Then the godfathers of Japanese hard rock.

'It was in Otaru, too, way up in the north. And it was almost New Year's.'

'Were they sloppy?' It seemed like something those guys would be. Sulking about having come to such an out-of-the-way dump. They had too much confidence in their own abilities. The lead guitar and bassist would switch instruments and totally mess about on stage.

'They were actually pretty good. Wildly jumping from song to song, one after the other. Their attitude was, like, doesn't matter if the audience don't get it.'

'Did any of them try it on with you?' I thought of Landi. I was sure he didn't waste any time back before he got married.

'I'm not you, Izumi.' She made a point of saying this. 'Also, no one talked much. It all felt very quiet, like everyone was cooped up inside themselves.'

Ai got up to go put a record on. Aretha Franklin came on.

'Hey, who told you?' I raised my voice slightly.

Ai glanced over at me as she put away the record that was on the turntable before.

'No one you know.' Her words were overly drawn out. She savoured every syllable as she spoke. Same as she did on stage. Her voice carried even when she spoke quietly.

'So I'm a demon witch, breaking up bands?' I pulled up my skirt and stroked my thighs.

'Haven't heard anyone say something like that in ages.' Even her smile was dripping with the blues. She couldn't help exuding melancholy, somehow.

'I never set out to do it on purpose, it's not even like I was always hanging out with the same band. It just ends up happening. Why not blame the guys who choose to be with me?'

I tried hugging in my thighs. With my short limbs, I looked like a silly child. Only my torso had matured.

'Don't you care about those poor legs of yours?' Ai's eyes dimmed.

'Nope, guess I am pretty rough with them.'

I let go of my thighs and pulled my skirt back into place. I leant against the back of the sofa.

'Bet all the boys butter you up, right?' She went into the kitchen.

'Yep. Wonder why,' I said idly.

Ai took two glasses down from a shelf. 'Gin and lime okay?'

I nodded. 'Just a dash of lime though. Too much makes me feel ill.'

'Chain of Fools' started playing. I listened. Aretha's strong, hearty voice resounded through Ai's pallid apartment and mixed with the sounds of the traffic below. It was like that all night there. A motorway was right next door. Maybe Ai was soothed by the noise of the city.

Another song began.

'It's one of the world's mysteries,' I said. 'I was talking about it the other day with a girl who gets around a bit. Why men always praise women's bodies.'

I heard clinking bottles and glasses.

'Women like me don't get praised,' Ai said.

I ignored her stiff comment and really thought about the phenomenon.

Then the sound of ice cubes.

'I don't have any lemons. You're fine without, right?'

'Yes,' I shouted back into the kitchen.

I listened to the record for a while.

It seemed downright fishy to me. Men didn't exactly take care to mind their manners in any other areas.

Ai appeared with a glass in each hand. I stood up and took one. Went back to the sofa, took a sip, then placed the drink on the table.

'Here's the conclusion we both came to. Maybe they're trying to convince themselves with those compliments. No man wants to think he's fucking an ugly girl.'

'Can't they tell?' She took a good swig of her drink.

'No, surely not. They don't know whether they're forcing themselves or whether they truly think it.'

'You're awful,' she said, gazing into her pale green glass. The ice cubes shifted slowly.

'Whatever gets said when you're in bed is like background music. It doesn't mean anything, really, as long as you're able to lose yourself somehow. I never believe a word.'

Another sip of gin. Aretha finished.

'What a sad way to think.' Ai smiled through her glass.

'Maybe. I try not to expect anything. I don't want to be disappointed later.'

'Why don't you stop going for the big shots?'

'Is that what people say I'm doing?' I asked.

'Yep. The members of that band are deluxe items, y'know.'

'I'm not interested in checking them all off.'

'Make do with the men around you. You're too idealistic.'

'Lately,' I said, pretending to pull my hair out, 'I tried giving one of the "men around me" a shot. Thought it'd be good to sample the ordinary for once. What happened? I got so bored. Ordinary equals no talent, nothing special, you see.'

'Not exciting enough?'

'Just so careless. No tact. Came out with such bullshit. And so suspicious, too. "You can't trust women," stuff like that. Why even bother with them then? One day he kept calling me again and again, from six at night right through to the morning. I couldn't deal with that. I didn't pick up. The sound of the phone ringing felt like a threat, riled me right up. I could still hear it even after I wrapped it in my duvet and shoved it in the closet.'

'He got obsessed, surely? It's you, after all.'

'Who knows.'

'I'm certain,' she said.

'The point is, he's insensitive. He couldn't get a handle on what I was feeling at all, so he'd say all this garbage, had all these stupid doubts. And yet, still so stubborn. I ended it, yuck. He's ugly inside.'

'You can do without that.'

'Yeah, right? Some people are beautiful inside no matter how dirty they act. Just a sliver of purity is fine. Even in men who treat me badly. Another thing: to my mind, anyone with talent can do whatever they like. I'll forgive them for it. I know that by extension that means people can do whatever, but still.'

'Anything goes.' Ai believed it too.

'Exactly – provided I can feel the beauty somewhere in what he's doing. If not, it's only natural I'll get fed up. That's why I've stopped seeing them, ordinary men.'

'I feel sorry for that guy. He probably doesn't understand why you dumped him, does he?' Not a scrap of empathy in her voice.

'He thinks it's to do with his looks. But that wasn't the only thing.'

'So appearance is a big factor too?'

'Obviously? Whoever said it took three days to get tired of a pretty boy was wrong. Even if he's not particularly expressive, he'll still have a range of poses and faces. So you're caught off-guard by his beauty each time you look at him. Spend half a day with a scruffy man and you'll catch a lot of disappointing angles.'

'You spoilt girl.'

'They say the uglies make up for it by being passionate and kind, but I don't buy that. I mean, what if someone does find them attractive, do they turn nasty then? Look, they're shabby and petty. And I can't speak for everyone, but in my experience, good-looking guys are good-natured. Pure and sincere. None of that needy defeatism, "I'm no good anyway," blah blah.'

'The only issue there is you'll have a lot of competition.'

'True,' I replied.

Ai's glass was empty. She fetched the ice bucket and the bottles of gin and lime cordial from the kitchen.

She put on another record. Some old folksy song. Young female singer, incredibly good voice. Vigorous and alive. I asked who it was.

'It's Misora Hibari.' Ai made dance-like gestures.

'Wow.'

'She's good, right?'

'Incredible.'

'So underrated, it's shocking. She's a singing legend.'

I nodded.

'Older records can be pretty interesting,' Ai said. 'Listen to the backing music.'

'Main thing is if the recording's good.'

'That doesn't bother me so much. As long as there's some soul in it.'

I was about to say something in response but I held back. Here we go, another serious person. To clarify, being 'serious' to me meant being logical about capability and power, which is why I disliked it. Maybe I'd feel differently if I were capable of doing something myself.

Ai asked me if I'd met so-and-so. The name went over my head. Nope, I said. No memory of him. But I was prone to forgetting people.

'Strange. He mentioned you. A girl called Izumi's into me,' he said.'

'No clue.'

'Maybe it's all in his head. Seemed pretty pleased about it, anyway. I'll introduce you.'

'What's he like?'

'Kind of outrageous.'

'Physique?'

'Similar height to you.'

'I'll pass, then.'

'Must be nice having all this choice.' Ai finished her second drink. I was trying to go slow. I knew that once I got to my fifth, I wouldn't stop.

'It does cost me,' I said.

'You mean you're too caught up in these romances to do any work?'

'Not just that. I was the same as a kid. I'd sacrifice anything if it earned me someone's love. Love was my reason for living. Not good, is it! Neurotic. I'm passive and dependent, I need people's love. Their doting love. Money or success mean nothing to me in comparison. I overvalue love.'

'It's okay, you're a girl.' Ai was kind.

I nodded.

'When I was in Kyoto recently,' she smiled with one corner of her mouth, 'my manager gave me a warning: I mustn't sleep with anyone. Just for one night. Kyoto's a college town, a pretty small place, right. Gossip spreads fast. If I'd slipped into some guy's bed for the night, come morning the whole town would be agog.'

She seemed to be enjoying herself. I reacted automatically to the mention of Kyoto. 'I called Joel,' I said.

'They've still not finished the first performance.'

I said I was calling from Tokyo. The staff member on the other end was friendly.

'Is it alright if I call back?'

'Sure. There's a break around nine o'clock.'

'Are they playing twice every night?'

'Three times on Sunday.'

What a tough gig. He used to be a megastar. Now his band's stuck in dance clubs. I said my thanks and hung up the phone.

I lay face down on the bed.

My left elbow and leg hurt. Bruises. Must've crashed into some furniture yesterday or the day before. I was drugged up to the eyeballs both days.

I'd run out of a certain pill so my nerves were shot. I had to go to Harajuku if I wanted to buy sleeping meds. That shop on the Meiji highroad would sell me anything.

I endured the dull pain for a while. I also had a headache, of course. My head ached all the time. I read in a magazine that people who get headaches tend to be selfish.

I was able to put up with it because I knew I was going to take some painkillers soon. Better than sleeping pills, I reasoned, indulging myself.

I stood up and pretended to be confused. Even though no one was watching. Decided to put on a record. The Doors, dark and sincere, too literary. I went for T. Rex.

I weaved back to the bed. Back to my previous posture. Before long (as expected) my arm stretched out and my hand picked up the long, slender cardboard box on my bedside table. The regular dose was two pills. Out of habit, I popped out four into my palm and washed them down my throat with some coffee dregs.

Ten minutes passed.

Electric sounds filled the room. This was a glam rock band I liked because they weren't about getting hyped up. They suited these sluggish, heavy moods.

The pain wouldn't go away. My headache felt even worse. I picked up the box and took two more pills. Whatever. The A-side finished. Two more.

That was it. Clean out of drugs that might soothe my nerves.

I checked the clock and got up. Put on a suit with nothing underneath. It being November, I planned to wear thigh-high boots.

I ran outside with my bag. A taxi stopped straight away. Traced the old sewage line to Tomigaya. On the left I saw the entrance to a Chinese restaurant called 'Other People'. What a name. Ranks high on my list of favourites. After the Clinic of Hope, the obstetrician's in Harajuku.

I carried on with these messy thoughts to trick myself. Huddled up in the dark backseat, I couldn't stop anticipating the drugs. The painkillers had already kicked in, but even so.

I stopped the taxi on the corner by the big Central Apartment shopping centre in Harajuku. I went into a pharmacy decked out with flashy displays of cosmetics. A blank-faced woman dressed in white appeared.

'Some Rislon and Optalidon.' My voice wavered a little. Without a word, she put two boxes in a paper bag.

'And one more of Optalidon.'

She didn't hesitate. I probably could have asked for another box of Rislon too. Well, never mind.

My stomach was unsettled. I had to eat something. I walked to a nearby café. Harajuku was quiet at night. I was glad. The lights studding the darkness seemed tasteful. It had been even more deserted when I lived in the area three years before.

I sat at a round table and asked for a gratin, like a child. A girl with green eyelashes was talking with a friend at the next table. She looked about fifteen or sixteen. A girl who looked older than that, with glitter in her hair, once told me she was fourteen. That one had also been wearing green eyeliner. I wonder where she'd got it. Blue or grey are easier to find. She talked about bands. A baby hard-rock chick.

The gratin hadn't arrived yet. I took four Rislon with a glass of water, and four of the pink ones too. I figured it wouldn't matter, if I ate soon after.

I asked Green Lashes for the time.

'Eight fifty-two.'

Less than fifteen minutes since I'd left the house to make my way here. I could probably use the café's phone. Too much effort to ask the waiter. I ate the whole gratin when it came. Went to pay as soon as I'd finished.

'See you next time,' she said.

I waved and left the café. I found a taxi straight away.

'I'm fed up of being here.' Joel sounded deflated on the phone.

'Doing the same thing every day?'

I was lying on my front on the bed. I'd come back home and taken four more Rislon. When I took pills here and there in bits and pieces like this, I would lose track of how many I'd downed in total.

'But we're still under contract.' The song requests didn't make it any better. Girls dropped by the dressing room during breaks. It was a claustrophobic, dirty little room just off the stage. Just a sofa and two broken chairs from the bar. Amps were kept in there, too. The air con didn't quite reach.

'There's nothing fun about it at all?' I thought my voice might tremble. I'd pictured him at the bottom of the stairs to the club with his bass by his knees.

'Nah.'

'What about the girls?'

'Well, dunno. Not exactly God's gifts. Why don't you come to Kyoto?'

'Me?'

'Yeah, I want to see you.'

He'd never said that to me before. I was happy.

'I'm scared of the other girls over there.' I'd be safe when I was with him. But when we were apart, I knew I'd be cross-examined by his Kyoto groupies. 'I don't know Kyoto, I don't have any money either.' Why was I refusing?

'Okay. Got it.' I couldn't tell if he was disappointed or not. Joel always sounded so cool and indifferent.

Maybe I'd just let slip some unfathomably important chance. The thought went through my head but the pain of it was faint. Nothing was direct. It felt like someone else's life. Everything felt like a plot line in a TV show.

'Alright, so when I'm back. You'll drink your fill. Just you wait, okay?'

I didn't understand what he said at first. His voice replayed in my head purely as sound. I heard myself say something that seemed like a goodbye. Joel responded and before I knew it the phone was dead.

I lay stupefied, alone in my flat. I'll call you. He'd said that, I remembered, after a while.

'What the hell did he mean?'

The same surprise, back at Ai's.

'What?'

She put out some little crackers and nuts in a wooden dish.

'Joel, with his "drink your fill" business.' Ai stood there eating the snacks.

'He meant exactly what it means, I expect.' I tipped my head to one side.

'Wait, it's that filthy?'

'Guess so.'

'As in, sexually?'

'Yes, of course.'

'That man's sure got some lines.' She finally smiled.

'I suppose.'

'An ordinary guy would never come up with that.'

'Pretty sure he just said it spontaneously, you know.'

'So bizarre. Usually it's something more vulgar, like "I won't let you sleep a wink".'

'It's because his brain's been hijacked.'

'Good man. It really hits home.' Ai was grinning.

'Yeah, it did hit home, three or four days later. Jury's still out on what it means *specifically*, though.'

Drink my fill of sperm. That's all I could think of, anyway.

'Like, what if he meant booze?' Ai laughed. 'Got hold of a goodie, haven't you?'

'I've not got a hold of anyone. We're not even dating.'

'Aren't you going to Kyoto?'

'I'm not sure enough about us. No one as pretty as him could fall for me. I can't imagine him even finding me mildly interesting.'

'You're pretty, too.'

'Please. His foot's better looking. Joel can take his pick. He's probably never had a girl turn him down in his life. Probably never even had to chase anyone. He's so passive, he was made that way, he's been put in this special world since his teens.'

Ai perched on the arm of the sofa. She clasped my head and asked gently, 'Why are you so insecure?'

'I've never been loved.'

'Honestly.'

'I'm serious.'

'No one's ever told you they loved you?'

'Oh yes, many times.' I sickened myself. I let men tell me anything, I let myself be taken in instantly, but in reality I didn't believe a word of it. 'I decided. Men are all talk.'

'But you know, even this Joel will get married at some point. No matter how pretty you say he is.'

'Yeah, probably. So surprising when totally expected things like that happen.'

'You will, too. Even you'll end up with someone.' Ai kept stroking my head.

'That someone can't exist, Ai.' Irrational, sure, but I firmly believed it.

'How come?'

'My head's not right. I'm fine with just the occasional hookup. But living together with someone would be impossible. He wouldn't be able to stand it. I always win the power games. So they feel like they've lost, and end up hating me.' That's what happened when I'd lived with a man before. He became spiteful and made everything my fault. *I'm a veteran*, he told me. *We're not in the same league. You're naked among wolves. Makes a higher being like me want to look away. I've experienced love and loss, I know despair. Now I just want to live a quiet life.* I still hated him.

'Intense, aren't you?' Ai smiled.

'Apparently. That man was jealous of how I existed.'

Ai moved away. She filled her glass with fresh ice and gin and drank. She seemed tired. She looked toward the window. 'You'll meet your match, I know it. He's out there.'

There was a constant stream of noise from the outside.

'Well, if he is . . .' I made myself a drink. My voice came out weirdly shaky. 'He's a complete lunatic, that's for sure.'

8

Time of the Season

I met Jun after a mistaken phone call. It was early December.

Some guy I didn't know was speaking to me with strange familiarity from the other end.

'I'm coming over now.' He was blunt from the start.

Looking back, I should have said no. My curiosity ruined me. I found his brashness, to suddenly say what he did, too interesting.

I got the call from outside the station just past eleven o'clock. I went down to meet him and was instantly disappointed. I'd pictured a pretty boy. But when I saw him I remembered; this was the guy Ai had offered to introduce me to, the one I'd turned down.

He was small, skinny, like a little schoolboy. Delicate frame and gentle, girlish hands. Egg-shaped, shy-looking face. Pouty lips, each side slanting upward. (I preferred a downward slant.)

When we got back to mine, he went straight to the bed. Sprawled out quite naturally. I was speechless.

Usually, if you were with someone you'd never met, you'd at least aim for a chair or something. In fact, you'd likely wait for whoever lived there to offer you a seat. I couldn't square Jun's cheek with his appearance. He looked like such a shy kid.

I pulled myself together and made some apple tea. I sat at the foot of the bed and spoke to him. He rested his chin on one arm and stared at me. His eyes were gentle, they had large pupils. Occasionally he laughed out loud. He seemed to find my expressions more interesting than my words. He was calm and unhurried, which put me on edge.

I lit one cigarette after another. Billowed smoke from my bright red lips. Like a real bad girl, don't mess with me, yada yada. Two puffs then I'd stump it out in the ashtray.

'So we're the same age. I'm third of May, so I'm like your older brother by two months and a week.'

He seemed pleased about that. He was even more pleased once he found out we were also the same blood type (AB).

'Why's your skin so green? Show me your arms,' I demanded.

He rolled up the sleeves of his jumper. Even his underarms had a greenish tinge.

'Wow, weird! You're the first person I've seen like this. Are you sick? Is it genetic?'

'I haven't slept for three days.' Jun smirked.

'And that's why? Can't be good, huh, if it's doing this to you.'

'I was working. I wanted to test how many songs I could come up with. Got to over a hundred.'

'On sheet music?'

'No, on my instruments.'

'You didn't write them down?'

'They're in my head. I never write music down. You only get one shot to win at free jazz.'

Jazz meant nothing to me.

'So your world's defined by victory and defeat,' I said.

'In a fight it's best to shrink your ground. That's why there's not much variation in my playing. I'm always squished in. I hate fake, impure sound. I only want to play clean and clear.'

'I love for things to be fake. It makes me happy. Makes me smile.'

'You're not thinking right. You don't take life seriously. With that mindset, sooner or later you'll fall apart.' Jun moved up and looked me directly in the face. It struck me how serious he was. He meant what he said. He was full of passion and energy. He used everything he had. I was impressed.

He grabbed my arm. 'What really matters is –'

'Can you not use that phrase? I hate it. It doesn't mean anything. People keep using it. Telling me what really matters. Actually, it's just marking out what *you* want to say. Also, telling me what's inevitable or absolute. It's all the same.'

I looked down at the arm he was holding. He noticed, apologised, let go.

'Chasing the absolute is my thing.'

This guy's not out of his cocoon yet, I thought. Psychologically uncircumcised.

'The absolute only exists conceptually. Like mathematics. Imaginary numbers.'

'I've been searching and chasing it for years. I want to get to the conclusion by the shortest route possible. Running faster than anyone else.'

'Try a bit of retrospective reasoning instead of chasing conclusions.' I said, smiling. 'It's easier.'

'You'll regret it sooner or later.' His warning seemed well-meant.

'I'll forget before then. It's one of my special skills. Forgetting, and giving up.'

'I've been trying to figure out why you're so calm about being so wrong when you're not stupid, and I've got it. What I have and you don't is persistence. Being stubborn is the best thing a person can be. You're not persistent enough.'

'Thanks.' I wondered if he lectured and preached at everyone like this.

'Wait, what?' He looked earnest. He waved his hands in the air.

Dawn was approaching.

'I'm sleepy.' I stood up.

'Come here, then,' he said. He made space beside him for me, as if it was his own bed. Made me feel like I was being a minor nuisance in his house.

I put on some nightwear and got in next to him. Turned out the lamp. The whitish light from outside filled the room like water.

He stroked me, like he was doing me a favour. He carried on. I wanted him to stop, really. Either that or be more sexual, speed it up, get excited, get it over with.

'Are you gay?' I asked, springing up. Maybe he was trying to hide it by pretending to be into women.

'No!' He got up too. 'I'll prove it to you.'

Jun pulled off my clothes in a controlled frenzy. His hands were swift and deft.

'No, come off it.' I tried to rebuff him. Had the sense a guy like this could kill a girl, despite the tame look in his eyes.

'It's not working.' His voice was frightening. He held my arms down with a strength I hadn't expected.

'Come on, that's enough. I get it.' I was honestly scared.

'I'll make you get it even more.' He looked down at my face from above. The eyelashes framing his drawn-out eyes seemed to shimmer.

'I'm sorry. I take it back. You're not gay. Okay?'

'Once I get mad I gotta do something violent.'

I gave up. I stopped moving. He yanked off his shorts.

Jun attempted coitus. However, his penis remained out of order. Sudden relief. I burst out laughing. Not at what had happened in itself, but out of relief.

I pointed and said, 'Look at that, Mr Limpy.'

Jun looked down between his legs.

'Weird. Maybe I'm too tired.'

'Often it just won't happen, right?' I was happy for some reason. No malice intended.

'No, it's not like that.' He seemed angry.

Here's one strange thing about men. Sometimes they can't get into it, they can't perform. Well, that's no problem. It's not like anything can be done about it. So why do they feel like it's some great shameful dishonour? Who am I to understand these things.

'It's fine, it doesn't matter.' I was still smiling. Found it endearing how serious he was being.

'It's not fine. My motto is "whenever, wherever, whoever".'

The silhouette of his torso with his back to the window wasn't as bad as when he was dressed. His chest was filled out, it must have measured ninety centimetres or so around. Didn't change the fact that he was skinny overall, though.

'Come on, it's fine.' I was relaxed. I put on my nightwear. Turned my back to him. Settled in to sleep.

'Hey, are you mad?' He hugged me from behind.

'Not at all.' I was sleepy, more than anything.

'Really?'

'Yeah.'

'Sorry.'

Why was he apologising? Made no sense. I couldn't be bothered with it so I just said, 'Got it.'

'Don't be moody.'

God. This time I didn't say anything back. He said it again.

'I'm not.'

He certainly was a stubborn bastard. He whipped himself up. He grumbled on for a while after that.

I went to sleep at six and woke up at seven.

I couldn't sleep any longer because Jun proclaimed loud and clear, 'Alright, wakey-wakey!' I wondered if he'd been like this all his life. Every time he woke up. I was surprised at myself, wondering about 'all his life'.

He stared at me with a cheerful look on his face. Then immediately pulled me to him.

'Stop it.'

'Why?'

'My body's not awake yet.'

'That's alright.' He took the liberty of deciding that.

He pressed his lips on my skin. Touched my breasts. His kisses and touches were soft. He went through the motions as gently as anything. But I could sense a ferocious brutality bubbling up beneath.

'Stop it,' I repeated. I hardly ever said that to the men I slept with.

'Why?'

'You're scaring me.'

'You were playing a right bitch yesterday. Cigarette hanging out the corner of your mouth. Like you were humouring a little boy. It was weird, I couldn't stand it. You saw through my show.' He snickered.

He pulled down his shorts. Slid his skinny body on top of mine.

'Stop, please.' I asked him one more time.

He opened those razor-blade eyes a little. A menacing look. I pushed away his hands, tried to push him off. Regardless he entered me, leaving no room for doubt about that.

I felt under attack. I couldn't pin it on anything in particular, but he was sadistic. Yet not violent. Like he was forcefully suppressing a strong excitement and behaving very coolly.

I turned my head to the side. I hated seeing cruelty. I threw up my arms, he grabbed my wrists and pinned me down. I wanted it to be over quickly.

He stopped moving. He rolled away, saying nothing.

'Did you come?' I asked, just to be sure.

'Yes. Inside you. No one realises at first. Positively middle-aged, the way I come.'

His expression was gentler. He looked sweeter than last night. Lighter.

'Didn't you feel it?' His voice had softened a lot.

'Nope.'

'Not at all? . . . Is it always like that?' He was being sensitive. I couldn't be bothered so I just nodded.

'You just haven't done it enough,' he said. 'Bet you've only slept with one or two other guys, right?'

I looked at him, dumbfounded.

'More like a hundred.' I couldn't say precisely. Might've been more.

'Seriously? I wouldn't have guessed, you know. If you'd said it hurt, most guys would've believed it was your very first time. You seemed just so scared. And also, here.' He pressed between my legs. 'Like a virgin.'

My face flushed red. When had he seen me down there?

'I feel bad for you, not feeling anything. With that cracking body of yours, too. I'd like to make you feel a bit more.'

In other words, Jun wanted to prove his manhood. It wasn't the moment to tell him how I did feel it with other men. Landi was one to remember.

Jun and I spent four days together. He stayed that night, went home the following day, then called me up in the evening. He was staying in his friends' flat in Yotsuya while they were away in Okinawa. I went to meet him there.

I could barely sleep or eat anything. My nerves had never been so twitchy around a particular man before. I didn't even

113

like him, it was a pain being with him, but I was drawn in by some strange power that he and no other man had. When I said I was going back to Yoyogi-Uehara he was only supposed to accompany me part-way, but he ended up coming back to mine again.

'Now's the time to say it. We're in love!' he proclaimed, quite seriously. 'I'll be with you for the rest of my life'. What was he thinking? He didn't even ask how I felt. No one had ever been this obsessed with me before.

Jun had fallen into a trap he'd set for himself. While striving to fix what he believed to be my problematic frigidity, he found himself caught by the very woman he was working on. Not that I ever really intended to catch him.

I myself didn't understand why I wanted to stir up a man I didn't even like.

Vanity before love. If a man's fit to show off to my friends, I'll keep him hanging. This one seemed clever, and more than anything he was brash and insistent. He's worth more if he's different.

No doubt this was the whore in me.

Jun's irritation was peaking. He'd spent too much time with the same person. We were waiting to cross the street east of Shinjuku station on our fifth night.

'Go away. Go!'

I tried to obey, but he pulled me back by the shoulders. He clung to me. He seemed angry and like he was crying.

'No, no. Why not?' He was talking to himself. He didn't want to let me go. Even though he'd had enough.

We walked around outside Kinokuniya without speaking. I wanted to push him over and run away. I wanted to change the situation. Anything would have been better than this.

'Let's get married. Okay?' Jun stood still.

'Sure,' I nodded without thinking about it.

'Right now!'

'It's the weekend, so we're too late. There's paperwork we have to prepare first. Let's get married on Monday.'

Jun was suddenly in a good mood. There was love and affection in the way he held me then, closer.

'You won't change your mind?' I asked, because I wanted him to change it. I'd started to regret it. Already.

'Never,' he replied, so quietly.

'I'll head over now, yeah?'

Saturday, as usual. Diana's lead guitarist on the telephone.

'I'm getting married.' I was looking at Jun. I wouldn't have said it if it weren't for him. Foo was quiet for a while.

'You quite sure?' he finally asked. Of course he'd find it hard to believe. I'd completely changed my mind in the space of a week. There'd been no warning signs. Foo, you're not the one. I hadn't properly told him my intentions.

'I'm with him now.'

I started to feel gloomy. The idea of getting married was terrifying, whoever it was to. The idea of surrendering everything to another person. To this person, especially. Who needs love if it means losing yourself inside it. Being loved is terrifying.

'Right. Well, that's great. Congrats.'

115

Twenty-year-old Mr Lead Guitar showed impeccable self-control. I never ended up hating or begrudging him. That's a rare thing. When I've been seeing someone for a while, they always lose their appeal sometime or other.

'I guess we can't meet up anymore, then. It's the end.' He spoke so gently. 'And I'd best not call you.'

I realised something shocking. Once I was married, I wouldn't be able to meet Joel after he got back from London.

'You can still call me. Even if it's nothing important.'

'Sure, but I'll try not to. It won't be good for your guy if I do. Well, I hope you'll be happy.'

The boy left the line.

For the first time ever, I'd done something that couldn't be undone. I looked over at Jun. To think I had to let go of everything for a man like him. If it was real, then our youth was over. I'd thought I would carry on forever without responsibilities.

Jun said nothing. He wrapped his arms around my shoulders. Pulled me close to him and stayed like that, silent. Maybe he was seeing what he was set to lose, too.

9

Can't Keep from Crying Sometimes

I opened the door for Etsuko and she hurried in to hold me, then drew back a little to take a look. At once her big eyes filled with tears.

'What the hell happened to you?'

I murmured something in response.

'You've lost so much weight! You look like an insect – like a dragonfly, with those goggly eyes sticking out of your head.'

I staggered to the kitchen table. Sometimes when I moved my vision went.

'How much do you weigh?' She put a bag from the supermarket on my table.

'Maybe thirty-eight kilos. This T-shirt is for eleven-year-old boys. Fits perfectly. The jeans are twenty-seven-inch and they're too big. I use a belt to keep them up.' I knew I was talking like a mental patient.

'What about your waist?'

'Down to fifty centimetres now.'

'Barely. God, I should've come sooner. I was worried about you but I've been so busy. I went stateside twice. I'm sorry.'

She took out some food and set it out on the wide table. She was clearly shocked. All there was in the kitchen was the table and a fridge. You couldn't see the few pots and pans we had because they were left in the sink in the wall.

In the next room there was just a phone on the floor. No curtains. Only the strip lighting, no lamps. The back room contained a wide and fruitless double bed.

'This is where you're living?'

She took out a paper cup (very well prepared) and poured in some milk.

'Jun wanted to live in Harajuku. It cost thousands just to move in. I used up all the savings from my modelling. But the rent's cheap, and —'

'You drink this. And you need something in your stomach. I bet you haven't eaten for days, have you?'

Etsuko was firm and kind. It was the first time in forever that I'd put something nutritious in my mouth. I'd forgotten what milk tasted like. Gluey and rich.

'Where's Jun?' She'd lowered her voice.

'Yesterday . . . I think it was yesterday, he came in the middle of the night, probably. He knocked and wanted to be let in. What did he say after that? Something about being worried about me . . . Then he kept talking out there, on and on, even after it got light. But I'm not sure, it might've been a dream. Seems like he was hanging about the area, though. I closed the shutters, you know, there was no way I'd let him in. I mean,

118

I'm . . .' But I suddenly had no idea what I was talking about. 'Lately I, the dreams I have, the hallucinations, my thoughts, I can't tell what's what sometimes.'

Etsuko sat on a chair at the corner of the table. She cocked her head to one side and asked, earnestly, 'You hate him that much?'

'I'll do anything to make him suffer. I'd even die. I've actually tried that already. While he was asleep I locked myself in the bathroom and used an old razor blade. Didn't hurt at all. Then for some reason he woke up. He smashed through the glass door and undid the lock inside to let himself in. He's got a mean left punch, you know. He planned to be a boxer before he got into free jazz. He took the razor blade and threw it out the window. Flew into a rage. If it gives him a hard time, I'll do it. Anything!'

Etsuko turned over my left wrist to see the scars. 'Why this, though? Doesn't he love you?'

'He says he loves me, so, so much!' There was an intense contempt in my voice. 'He gets annoyed if we're not together every minute, he hates it, he even tries to drag me along to work, he won't let me be alone, he watches me constantly. He's not right in the head. How can someone be so clingy and persistent? When we're together he nitpicks about everything, he's never satisfied, if I say something in a way he even only slightly dislikes, he chases it tirelessly, so stubbornly you wouldn't believe, he says he lives by the premise that he's right about everything. He says I'm his now because he sacrificed everything to get married, I'm all his, down to every last hair on my head.' The longer I spoke the angrier I felt.

119

'Freud would have a field day. It's the Oedipus complex. He was totally doted on by his mother, now he's just put you where she used to be,' Etsuko said.

She'd only met Jun once. Before that she'd seen him play at the Pit Inn. 'A hysteric,' was her verdict.

'He's genuinely mentally ill. He has an epileptic fit once a week. I reckon it's because of all the drugs he takes, he's an addict.' I'd looked it up in a medical textbook. Epileptics are stubborn and easily angered. They're slow. Usually lethargic and slovenly. Their energy builds up and suddenly explodes.

'If I make some spaghetti, will you eat it?' Etsuko was holding my hands.

'Dunno. Do I have to?'

She nodded.

'Okay, I will.'

She got to work with what few utensils we had.

'It's not as bad as for you, but I'm not exactly happy myself, either.' She sat back down and went on talking as she waited for the water to boil. 'If I have a choice between two options, I'll always choose the worse one. I moan when it doesn't go well but I'm actually rather glad about it. I'm collecting proof for myself that the world is cruel, I've been dealt a bad hand, grim things always happen to me. I just hinder myself, I set up these obstacles.'

'I love you.' I clung to her arm.

'I love you too. Well, after going through the same failures over and over I realised that maybe I hate happiness, maybe I loathe it. I'm getting married and moving to the States soon, but I don't love him, Pete, at all.'

'Pete? The black bassist guy?'

'Remember when I was heartbroken over Johnny. They used to be in a band together, so I talked to Pete about him. He was kind, he sympathised. I wanted a clean break, I'd had enough. He asked me to marry him, so that's what I'm doing. I'm tired of being alone, spending all this time just with my own miserable self.'

'So you're going to spend time with someone else's miserable self.'

We were both quiet for a while. Etsuko went and put the pasta in the pot.

'Your husband, Jun I mean, he really has a gift. When he plays sax he chases himself to the very limit, right to the border between life and death. Nothing else matters. People like that shouldn't get married.'

She turned around. 'Least of all to someone like you.' She turned back to watch the pot.

'Still, couldn't you have done something else? Rather than lock him out and starve yourself. I guess not. This is the most you can do to reject someone who aspires to never leave your side.'

'I didn't expect he'd be this crazy.' I was fishing for her affection.

'Me neither. He makes this dark, scary impression but he treated you with extreme care. I thought he was being kind. Guess I was wrong.'

'But he does mean well. When I'm sick he sits beside me and asks every five minutes if I'm okay, repeats that he's with me, urges me to pull myself together. I get so moody. Then he grows sleepy once it's late, he falls asleep. Yet he'd just been stopping me from getting any sleep. So then I'm furious, so mad I have even less chance of sleeping. That's just one example, but . . .'

Etsuko used a towel to open a heated can of bolognese sauce. She brought two plates to the table.

'You fixed the broken door you mentioned on the phone, right?'

We ate sitting opposite each other. I managed to put food in my mouth with Etsuko here.

'That was two weeks ago already. Jun's friend came round and they both went to a café. I locked the door straight away, he kicked up a fuss, yelling at me to open the door. It's made of wood, he spent half an hour bashing a hole through it. His fists were covered in blood. He couldn't play for a while after that. I call him the "Emperor of Destruction". Oh, and I trembled when he smashed my Green Glass LPs, before. Guess that was just the intro.'

'When was that?' Etsuko stopped moving her fork.

'We went to Kyoto ten days after we'd met. So, last year. He stole the money for the trip from the woman he'd been living with until then. I only found out after, from her. Jun was in great spirits in Kyoto, even with me talking nonstop about Joel.'

'He knows about Joel?'

'I've told him about all the men I've been with, the ones I remember, anyway. I was frank about it. It wasn't a great idea. Whipped up his fighting instinct and need for conquest. Only further solidified his resolve to stick with me 'til death do us part.'

Etsuko sighed. She looked up at the ceiling. 'Surely you didn't give him all the details you've given me?'

'I gave him more.'

'Most people would try and keep that stuff secret.'

'But he wanted to hear it. He looked happy when I was telling him.'

I ate my meal properly.

'Did you tell him what Landi did with you? How you like Chinese men because they're such filthy bastards in bed?'

'Yes. I hoped he'd hate me and call off getting married. It had the opposite effect. In Kyoto he was flapping his arms about like a duck, grinning and asking what Joel did next. But once we got back home he was smashing up records for hours. All my Western music went.'

'So stupid, the pair of you.'

'Yep.' I finished the spaghetti. 'Yokohama's so close, after all, just a train ride away. Plus he probably wants to block out any voices other than his own.'

The phone rang in the middle room. I jumped and grabbed Etsuko's arm. She seemed surprised by how shaken I was. She held my shoulders down. The phone rang exactly thirty times, so for a full minute and a half, before it stopped.

'He's coming, he's coming! What should we do? Oh, I hate this. I'm so scared.' I felt I was going to have a panic attack.

'You're like an abused child. Come on, keep still.'

'I can't. He's trying to swallow me whole. That's what I'm scared of.'

The phone rang again. I held my head in my hands, screamed soundlessly, tugged at my hair.

'Let's go somewhere else. Just for a while. Come on, it's okay. Give me your key. I'll make sure he can't get inside the house, okay? He doesn't have a key, does he? Good. You don't need to be afraid now.'

She held me and led me outside. I was light-headed with the hurrying. The blood drained from my head and everything went dark. I'd fainted on the pavement. Etsuko took me to a café nearby.

She took a sip of iced coffee. 'Does that happen often?'

I stared out the window. Fluttering clothes in the glaring sunlight were floating along the pavement like phantoms.

'I was shocked. You were out cold for half a minute.'

It took a while, around a second or two, after the words were uttered before I understood what she was saying. I got so dazed sometimes.

'Not always that bad,' I replied.

Harajuku felt stained now. It was such a quiet neighbourhood when I'd lived there in 1970.

'You really do sound like a child when you're speaking, sweetheart. Like you're trying your best to speak properly but your brain's just not caught up yet. Your pronunciation, it's like you're a little girl.'

It had been even worse several weeks back. I couldn't even speak. I'd regressed that far in the space of half a day. I crawled around the flat on all fours. I couldn't go to the toilet by myself. Jun had to take me and hold me from behind to get me to pee, like a baby. He put me in the bath and lifted my arms up, one then the other, giving me a wash. I stood up dripping and he dried me with a towel.

124

He lifted me up and put me in bed. I weighed so little, after all. I didn't mind being touched, but once it became sexual, I shrieked. That's what was scariest to me, more than hating or getting sick of Jun. No longer being able to have sex like a proper adult. Memories came back to me with ferocious intensity, of guys in the neighbourhood playing tricks on me as a kid.

I can't masturbate, he once told me. *Never done it once, not my whole life. That was the hardest thing when I got held in a detention centre for a week. If you won't let me do it with you, I'll have to find it somewhere else.* Then, when he tried again: *Once you're married, you can't cheat. I mean, it's a holy covenant. A promise is between people, right? But a covenant is made with God. So even if no one sees and no one knows, it can never be broken. That's how sacred it is. So how dare you make me go and sleep with other women.*

I'd banished him from my bed. I was terrifically happy at the thought of his libido being discharged elsewhere.

Etsuko was quiet for a moment. We both looked out of the window together.

'I never knew it would end.' That's right. She'd been thinking the same as me. 'We were so young. Those days will never come back. I know that sounds like a line from some drippy ballad.'

I said nothing. I could sense that time, out there through the window. We're on our way to hear a band, I'm messing about with a guy. An echo-chamber pedal plugged into the night, the reverb coming back vividly enough to squeeze the blood from my heart.

'Foo and Joel.' She looked at me once she'd said their names. Smiled faintly. 'I wonder what those two are up to now.'

I took both her hands in mine on the table.

The last time Foo phoned me was early one evening, two and a half months after I told him I was getting married.

'You doing well?' He didn't sound on top form himself.

'Not especially.'

'I'm at Tokyo Station. About to head home.'

'Okay.'

Jun was listening. His face arranged to look casual.

'So this is how it ends, huh.'

Don't say that. My regret only swelled.

'Aren't you seeing anyone new?'

Jun made strange gestures with his hands. I made a guess and reached for the tin of Peace cigarettes (even though he was closer to it), lit one for myself, put one in his mouth and lit that too. I'd never been with a man who was so much hassle. I even shaved him in the morning. He'd asked and asked, so persistently. He made the same demand no matter how many times I refused. In the end I got sick of saying no. And to think how I hated it, looking after people like that. That's how he got me to do it.

Foo sighed. 'I've just been sleeping around.'

'I'm sure there are other girls you'll like.'

'I s'pose so.' Hearing him speak like that, I felt like leaving Jun. 'Work's no fun either,' said Mr Lead Guitar. 'I'll never forget you, you know. You were always so kind with me. Always.'

'I should be saying that to you.' I knew it wasn't advisable to get emotional. Not in the circumstances we were in.

'You're a woman to remember. Well, I have to get my train. This is goodbye then.'

'Goodbye.'

He put the phone down.

Foo had no intention of calling me again. He didn't think he was allowed to anymore.

'Come here,' Jun said. I was hunched over. He sounded weirdly gentle. I did as I was told. He hugged me. He said things like, 'He really did love you so much, didn't he.' And I could hear it in his voice: Jun was comforted by the thought that he was the better man after all. Drunk on his own victory. How lame, getting off on something like that.

My Diana LPs had already been destroyed, long ago.

'I'll be living in California,' said Etsuko. I shuddered. All the feelings I'd lost began to stir again once I looked at her. Then they got stronger. Even in the short space of time we sat facing each other. 'That's just the way it is, I guess.' The border between her big pupils and the whites of her eyes was blurring. I couldn't say anything, only shake my head.

'Don't cry. Listen, I'll write to you.' Etsuko had tears in her eyes. We both sat still for a long time.

It was early evening once again and I was in bed. I heard a faint sound from the porch. Jun, coming home for the first time in four days. I'd let my guard down and forgotten to lock the door. He seemed to be unpacking things in the kitchen. He was strangely quiet today. I could hear his breathing. He drank some water.

He entered the gloom of the far room, where I lay. He stood next to the bed. I turned around and looked up at him. The Mitsubishi Heavy Industries head office was bombed yesterday. I wasn't sure why, but I got the sense that Jun was involved somehow. The police might come, they might take him away.

He sighed again. He got into bed. He pulled over a blanket and stretched out next to me. He looked up at the ceiling for a while. The curtainless window was wide open, letting a breeze in. It wasn't particularly hot. Shrubs had grown around the window, obscuring the view from outside. The leaves rustled.

'A building got blown up, didn't it.'

'Yeah,' Jun replied dimly. Both his arms crossed high on his chest. 'How did you know? You don't watch TV, you never see anyone.'

'Etsuko told me.'

He turned to face me. 'She was here today?'

I nodded.

'Bet she was shocked to see you, right?' He looked back up to the ceiling again. 'I might know the guys who did the bombing.'

Since the late sixties Jun had been popular with student 'extremists'. He said he often used to play at college festivals. 'One faction invites me to play. Then another opposing faction wants me to perform for them. I end up saying yes to both. I have no integrity, after all. I once got punched right in the middle of my solo. Ever since that, I've been playing with my eyes very slightly open. To watch out for the audience.'

I didn't believe everything he said. He definitely had delusions. For someone so overly sensitive to other people's moods and feelings, he was capable of some wild misunderstandings.

Not because he wasn't intelligent. He just went funny in the head sometimes.

'Izumi,' he called.

'Yeah.'

'Come here, show me your body.' He spoke like a parent. I looked down and undid the buttons on the set of kids' pyjamas I was wearing. He helped me take them off.

'Look at this.' He ran a critical eye over my protruding rib cage. 'Your back's like a washboard. Bones sticking out all over the place.' He held up my breasts with one hand. They hadn't shrunk as much as the other parts, still a little more than his hand could hold. 'I've been worried the whole time. Every other day I stood there by the door. Once I spent three or four hours trying to get what was going on inside. I don't think you noticed.'

For a man, Jun was deeply caring about people. Excessively kind. That's why he couldn't see things impartially. If someone ran into a problem, he would empathise with the circumstances far too much. If two people were arguing, he sided with whoever he felt closest to. He never thought about who was actually right.

'If this carries on you'll die.'

He really was worried. But that's because he didn't have another ready object to consume his emotional energy. His emotions were being stimulated by something else, some-where else. He wanted to expend them using the safest method available.

'You're being so brazen, showing off this attitude like how you could live perfectly well without me. You're plotting and scheming, trying to break up with me, saying things to your friends. What's worse is that even though you do understand me, you pretend you don't. When you understand it all. You understand that all I am is me, nothing more. But because it doesn't suit you, you pretend not to understand. That's what sets you apart from other girls and it's just awful. Other girls never understand me, you see. They all just enjoy their delusions. Whereas you have the ability to understand me. You wield it like some kind of privilege.'

He was using his Serious Topic voice. I cocked my head to one side and listened carefully to what he said. I still hadn't put my pyjamas back on.

'I knew you didn't have feelings for me. The reason I still got together with you was because I thought I'd never meet anyone else like you if we let each other go. You have so much energy. It's concentrated and focused, too. Like drilling through a wall of concrete. And why? Because you're insane.'

I pulled a blanket up to my chest. I was feeling a little cold. Even though it was the middle of August. I got chills sometimes. I'd lost so much weight, so quickly.

Jun glanced at me calmly. He went on: 'Maybe I've been too sincere.'

You could say that again. Jun was highly-strung. I found it hilarious at first. The misunderstandings were so funny. Far funnier than planned misunderstandings, like jokes and gags, is when someone ends up being misunderstood by mistake. Let's say they wear an outfit they think is stylish and fashionable, but which to other people looks hopelessly lame. That's way more amusing than if they'd worn a weird outfit on purpose. Cheers me up.

But Jun's self-belief was as unshakeable as an aching back tooth. Brush it slightly, tease him just a little, and his reaction would be fierce. He'd insist he was right. His rock-solid resistance was due to the severity of his condition. His illness had progressed beyond hope.

I decided I wouldn't play along anymore since he'd lost his mind. He wasn't happy about that. He wouldn't accept my lack of interest. He got angry if I wasn't sharply focused when we were together, got grumpy if I even looked at a vase of flowers instead of him. Like I had to always, and forever, be earnestly paying him attention. Total devotion to my husband. There was no room for joking about. He had a serious disorder. He wanted to swallow up the entire world. That's how hungry he was.

'I wasn't amused when you started with your panic attacks. At such tiny things, too. Being in love isn't supposed to be easy breezy, you know. If I told you to die, you should be willing to die, without even asking for a reason. That's how it must be.'

I wasn't in love at all. I wondered how he'd reached that misunderstanding. And those conditions were far too demanding.

'Your hysterical episodes only got worse. There was no limit. You went as good as blind. You didn't want to see the man you hated, and your hatred was absolutely thorough. That's what made it clear that you're an even more sincere person than me.'

Just being sincere isn't enough, I thought. There needs to be humour. If you forget about having a laugh and get too caught up in the details, you only get weirder, things only get more and more unusual. Well, nothing wrong with that, but . . . it's tiring. Truly, I was so tired. I was tired even of hating Jun. I no longer cared. My life was over. Because Joel didn't like me. It seemed that being jilted had made me feel let down, so I ended up clinging to this man here. If only I hadn't been so desperate then, when I couldn't see Joel anymore, when Jun was being so persistent. But it was too late.

'Look, you will literally die if you go on like this. Not that you seem fazed by that at all.' He hadn't spoken to me this nicely in weeks.

'I ate today,' I said. 'A proper meal.'

He looked at me searchingly. He thought I might be fibbing to make him feel better. I'd pretended to eat before. Hidden food, thrown it up.

'Etsuko brought food for me. She cooked for me, that's why.' No change to my infantilised psyche.

'So you're going to eat properly from now on?'

'Yes.'

'Whether I'm with you or not.'

I nodded.

'That's a good girl.' He patted me on the head.

I felt disappointed. 'You don't hate me?'

If only he hated me. Then I'd make love with somebody somewhere else, we'd hold each other fiercely without speaking a word.

'I don't hate you.' The answer I expected.

Why was he so attached to me? It was such a mystery. Maybe it was because I tickled parts of his psyche. That Oedipus complex Etsuko mentioned, for instance. My arms were just

132

bones. I wrapped them around Jun's neck. He held me softly. He let go and gazed at me, face to face.

In some parallel world I was still single, chasing pleasure day in day out. Maybe I'd have gone to Kyoto to see Joel that last time. I just couldn't let it go. Not the idea of being with Joel, no. I mean those days, that life.

I could hear some Dixieland jazz playing through the French windows of the neighbouring building. A cat and a woman lived there. Jun was watching me with a serious look on his face. He leaned over me. My body was in a limp, crumpled-up posture. He slowly brought his face closer to mine. I closed my eyes. It had been an age since we last kissed. His lips moved slightly, gently. When his tongue crept in I tried to push him away. He sensed it and put his hands on my shoulders to reassure me. I was still shaking after he pulled away. My heart was twitching.

'Did that scare you?'

'A bit,' I said.

The song was 'St James Infirmary'. It's about a pimp talking to a dying prostitute. You'll never meet a man like me in heaven, he says, so you better not die.

Jun laughed. 'You're like a teenager. Even most teenagers wouldn't act like this.'

'But . . .' I pressed the left side of my chest. I could hear voices from the house with the French windows. Couldn't make out what they were saying. Sounded like a man had come to visit.

Jun laid me down. He kissed me again, and this time it felt sexual.

133

'Can I?' He asked. I nodded. He took our clothes off. We were stark naked.

The night thickened. A faint indistinct light from the clear sky outside filtered through the gauze of window shrubs and spread inside. He tried putting it in. It hurt. It wouldn't go in.

'What's wrong?' Jun frowned. 'Is something different?'

'It's fine. Do it.'

He tried. 'I can't. You're all closed up.'

'Doesn't it feel a bit weird to you?' Because I'm so skeletal.

'Yeah, sort of. I mean, it feels like I'm doing something bad. What if I do something and because of the physical shock you end up dying from a heart attack or something.' He spoke so pitifully. 'It feels as if a hug would kill you.'

'Doesn't it turn you on? Like, sadistically?'

'Not when it's this bad.'

I could hear 'California Dreamin''. I thought of Etsuko straight away. She was far from dreaming about it. She'd already left. Jun kissed me. Then he tried to put it in again. Etsuko had left. We'd quietly confirmed that our time together was over. Jun was putting all his strength into it. 'It hurts,' I grimaced. He moved about. Other men would have at least used some spit. 'It hurts!' I threw my head back to try and escape from the pain. Still, he eventually fit inside.

'You're bone-dry,' he whispered into my neck. 'But I fit just right inside you.'

The Mamas & the Papas ended their melancholy chorus. 'Time of the Season' by The Zombies started up. Sounded like the music was on tape. Must've ripped it from the radio. Jun started moving back and forth again. I felt like I was sleeping with a guy for the first time in my life. Like I was offering up my body, devotionally. I shed tears. He stared right at me the entire time. His long-tapering eyes were dim and beautiful.

'This looks painful. I'll finish quick.'

I nodded and closed my eyes.

'Hold me,' he said. I lightly wrapped my arms around his back. I could tell when he ejaculated. We were fused together that snugly. Fluid filled the space between our bodies. He was still for just a moment before carefully detaching himself. He put an arm around my back and held me firmly. I'd shrunk so much that I fit completely within his stick-thin arm.

'You surprised me,' he said, looking at me from above. 'Not because you let me in. I always thought that'd happen eventually. I meant, the way you became like a virgin again. Most girls aren't even that timid their first time. You're so skinny, too, that there was absolutely no feeling of any fleshly body there. Nothing but your psyche there underneath me. The old Izumi is dead and a new woman has been born. A woman to live forever with me.'

We stayed in bed, didn't turn on the lights. It hurt until after the fourth time.

'You must be exhausted, surely?' Jun got up.

'Yes. But I didn't feel anything.'

'Just like your first time. Too scared. Plus you're not even into me, not one bit.'

'I like you now.' I was embarrassed for some reason. 'I like you almost too much.'

'Alright.'

Etsuko had helped him out. I wonder if he knew that. If she hadn't mentioned Foo and Joel (and Landi) to me, maybe none of this would have happened.

'Let's get something to eat,' he said. He pulled me up. My chest was soaked. 'This isn't your sweat, huh. It came from me.'

I showered and put on a red escargot skirt. Jun told me to doll myself up. I put on some light makeup. I fleshed out my face with some blusher I'd never used before. Jun asked if I could walk. I could. We held hands and walked to Aoyama.

We were eating clam chowder. I suddenly thought how terrifyingly momentous it was for people to live their lives loving each other. I still didn't love the man before me, though. I still hadn't ever loved anybody.

'What's wrong?' Jun noticed my spoon had stopped moving.

I shook my head. Suddenly nothing remained of the desire I'd just felt to become one with another. I thought, what a terrifying thing this marriage will become.

10

Loveless World

I woke up immediately at the sound of light footsteps coming up the stairs. I looked at the cot in the darkness. The baby seemed to be fast asleep. I went to the door without turning on the lights.

Jun had been somewhere else for about a week. He was gone for two months towards the end of my pregnancy. He came and went erratically and without notice. Yet there I was despite it all, still so sensitive to my husband's return, even while I was asleep. I hated myself for it.

I opened the door before Jun knocked. He was carrying instruments in both hands. He looked very haggard and pale. Like a dead person. It was the drugs he'd been abusing since the age of fourteen. His skin looked green when he was tired. Green eyes were prettier than green skin. (All that was so long, long ago.)

We looked at each other and before we'd said anything I began to feel hostile. I moved away from the door, turned my back to him and crossed my arms. I held each of my elbows in my hands.

Jun put his instruments down. He was tensing again. Let's call it the grumps that come with epilepsy.

'What's that look for?' He threw some fighting words out there but didn't seem too confident tonight.

I turned back around. He was still standing there.

'I'm tired,' he said, aimlessly. He took a pack of filterless Peace cigarettes from his trouser pocket and lit one. He sat down.

'Why, been having too much fun?' I couldn't help being harsh.

'Is that all you've got to say to me?'

'Nobu phoned. She was pretty irate with me. You're his wife and you don't even know where he is, she said.'

'I'm sick of her.' Jun frowned. 'Why's she so bloody persistent?'

'She's like that because of you. She came over here uninvited, stayed for three weeks and you just allowed it. You're both absolute psychos. It's a perfect match. Two hyperactive peas in a pod.'

'You don't really think that.' There was a twitch under one of Jun's eyes. Maybe he'll hit me, I thought. Well, fine. Thirty-odd times in an ambulance still hadn't done anything to change me. I knew that using violence meant you'd lost.

'I hate this,' Jun said. He sounded oddly delicate. 'I know it's probably mostly my fault. But I hate it, living in hell like this.'

'Well . . .' I adopted a gentler tone. I sat next to him, looked him straight in the face, and tried to talk him round. 'Then let's not do it anymore.'

'Here we go again. Break up, is that the only option? There's nothing else?'

Jun went as far as he could, then when he was all tired out and weak he'd come back home, and he believed, however irrationally, that no matter how terrible his behaviour was, no matter what he did, I'd forgive him, I'd take him in, and I'd even console him.

'No,' I said coolly.

'The reason I can't be nice to you anymore is because I've been sleeping with so many other women. I've slept with so many by now that it's not even like I'm cheating on you. It's just normal.' Incredible logic. But he was saying what he truly believed. That was clear. 'I've found myself getting attached. It's hard to break something once it's formed. It's not just one or two women, either.'

'So? What about me then, what should I do?'

He looked at the floor and was quiet for a while. Jun had small facial features but a large skull. In certain lights it could look like he had a massive brain. He shook his big head. 'You should know that yourself.'

Bullshit. I didn't need groundless faith like that. Jun always wanted to throw his weight around. Behave like a domineering tyrant with me. But subconsciously he also wanted the same subordinate woman to completely control him.

'I don't want to ever do anything for you again.' I spoke from the heart. How many times had we had this conversation? Each time I thought it'd be our final breakup chat. Then three years would pass. I felt powerless more than anything.

'Is it too late?' he asked.

'Probably.'

His head hung lower and lower. He hunched his back, his neck jutted forwards, he sat there deflated. He was so scrawny all over, he looked so feeble. Of course, it was just for show. But it still pained me.

'Look, you should go to bed.' I played along, speaking to him gently.

'Okay.' He leaned his head over. I stroked it.

'Have a pee first, okay?'

He nodded. This was the treatment Jun wanted lately. So I'd issue little orders like this now and then.

'I'll be back in a bit.' He stood up and turned around.

He always did that now. Before he went to the toilet, before he went to sleep, before he ate – anything. He always tried to get my permission first. Not in front of other people, of course.

I thought it was so stupid. He wasn't a little schoolboy. I'd ended up with a ridiculous handful of a man. I hated it. I hated taking care of men. Absolutely hated it. Clingy, close relationships made me feel nauseous. Be it with family or friends, I preferred crisp, fresh indifference. I'd simply given in to his demands. I'd just got sick of saying no.

Jun came back from the toilet. 'Hey, give me a shave.'

'Get another girl to do it, if you don't want to do it yourself.' I think I shot him a pretty frank look.

'I'm telling you to do it for me!' His face went red.

The smallest thing set him off. It wasn't normal. I thought he was mentally ill but his mother, sister and Nobu all said he wasn't. Being so attached, they'd lost the ability to judge. I was no match for such a pushy opponent. I began the shaving prep.

Jun loved me, like he said. Except his way of loving was

140

different to other men's. He completely ignored my wishes and well-being. He didn't think we were different people with different feelings in the first place. He might have had an inkling about it but he wouldn't want to acknowledge it. Jun wanted to believe that we were both one, of the same flesh.

He had no qualms reading letters that were addressed to me. He read my journals and if I'd written something he didn't like, he'd rip the page out. If he slept with another woman and enjoyed it, he came home and delivered a finely-detailed report. Because that joy should be shared, he explained to me one day. From that point on, I knew he wasn't right in the head. On what planet would a woman join her husband in being happy about his love affairs?

'Come here.' I beckoned him over.

'Okay.' Jun sat obediently in a chair. I pressed a hot towel to his cheeks and got the shaving cream ready. I moved close and carefully shaved his facial hair. I wondered how he could be so placid. Didn't he consider that his wife, with a razor in her hands, might hurt him? We had such fierce fights. I found his trust annoying. I finished shaving him and wiped up with the towel.

'I just remembered something Etsuko wrote in a letter. She said her kid glares exactly the way you do. Then she said she thought you were like an infant.' I was grinning.

'Bullshit!' Jun turned his head. He took the towel from me and wiped himself down. 'That's what's stupid about her. You're an idiot as well for taking it seriously.'

I didn't answer. When Jun was riled up, I usually wanted to egg him on. And that's what I'd do. He always responded to my provocations. Wonder why he never saw through it. It was so simple. But this time I was too tired.

'Your stupid shit drives me nuts!' He threw away the towel and went towards the bed, got in and turned his back to me. He was luring me in.

I cleared up the shaving gear and got into bed next to him. 'Hey, hey.' There was a necessary set of procedures to follow to restore his pride. If that isn't infantile, I don't know what is. 'I didn't mean to make you angry.' No? What did I mean to do, then? Whatever. This is no occasion for logical consistency. 'I'm glad you're back.' What a vapid thing to say. 'So turn to face me,' I continued.

'You want me to face you?'

'Yeah.'

'Did you miss me while I was gone?' Like a soppy teenager. Not a scrap of embarrassment about coming out with a line like that.

'Oh, so much.' Bravo, bravo. Guess I'm one to talk. 'I'm serious, I want you to face me.'

'Okay.' He turned over. I was shocked. Usually he'd be grinning. Maybe he'd intended a grin this time, too, but his face looked strangely gaunt and drawn. His eyes didn't look right. As though his pupils had sunk too far down. Somehow I knew it. I knew he was far, far gone.

'What's wrong?' Jun was trying to smile. It looked creepy.

He did go to sleep, eventually. But I stayed wide awake after seeing that.

'There. The old lady, sitting there. She's looking at me.'

My fears were realised the next day. Jun had started seeing things.

'There's no one there, Jun.'

'There is. She's there. She's looking at me.'

Maybe he's just worn out, I thought. I had to get him to rest. But how? There was no way in hell sleeping pills would work on him anymore.

'Look, there too! There's a man there. He's looking at me too.'

Even tranquillisers were hopeless now. A psychiatrist was probably the best bet. His pupils had sunk down even lower than they were the night before. I could only see the top half of them, giving him a bizarre, unreadable expression. Two stars sinking below the horizon at dusk.

'No, the kid's going to die! I've gotta help her!'

He ran to the built-in closet and opened up all the drawers. There were skirts and pillows near the bottom.

'There, there. Good girl.' Jun was holding and rocking a little body that wasn't there. He seemed to be acting on a stage. His hallucinations meant he could feel the weight of the body. 'It's alright now.' Going insane hadn't changed his goodwill. Jun sincerely wanted to be there for others.

He began to tip over sideways. His face froze as he fell. It was completely still. A seizure was coming. After a breath, he began having an epileptic fit. His whole body spasmed. He bared his teeth. His eyes were open so wide they looked about to pop out.

I closed the curtains. Light and sound only intensified the seizures. He was moaning and spasming violently. His voice was so awful. He wasn't conscious. It continued for a minute. Longer than usual.

The convulsions began to ease. Jun frothed at the mouth. He was suddenly breathing very hard. He didn't breathe during the seizures. His brain didn't get any oxygen then. His mental faculties were fading faster as the seizures grew more frequent, I was sure of it. Each one killed a load of brain cells. By then, Jun struck me as a lot dumber than he did when we first met. It can't have been just because I'd grown used to him.

I wiped around his mouth with a towel. His face was pale and he had burst into a sweat, which always happened after a fit. This time he wasn't vomiting, but only because he hadn't eaten since the day before. The tension drained from his limbs. He slowly closed his eyes. I thought he might go to sleep. Often he'd be tired out and end up dropping off. He opened his eyes slightly.

I took off his clothes. His arms and legs were completely limp and heavy now. He was like a doll. His entire body was drenched in sweat. I wiped him down with a damp towel. I dressed him in some dry clothes.

He had three seizures.

Even well into the night, he couldn't sleep. He sat in a corner of the room, hugging his knees.

The phone rang. Jun jumped. It was Nobu. 'I can't be dealing with you,' she snapped at me.

I was tired. 'Jun's gone mad,' I said softly.

'What?' She was four years younger. She put all her might into getting outraged.

'Well,' I added, 'he must've already been mad ages ago to waste any time with you.'

'What did you say? You trying to be funny?'

Nobu easily flew off the handle. Especially since things had turned sour between her and Jun. She'd faked her own death six or seven times already to try and get his attention. I liked to call her a 'sham-suicide virtuoso'.

'I don't have time for this,' I said. 'I'm hanging up.'

'Put him on the phone!' She was yelling.

'Best not to get him agitated.'

'You're jealous, aren't you? Jealous of us. You're trying to get in the way, aren't you?'

I'd almost rather die than talk to such a halfwit. I wondered if she ever realised how bizarre the things she said were. 'Wouldn't most people? If your husband was seeing another woman? Most people would try and get in the way. Not that I ever have.'

'Put him on! I'll judge for myself how bad a state he's in.'

I waved him over. I handed him the receiver, saying it was Nobu. He didn't look convinced. He took the receiver quietly. It seemed he was losing his willpower as he worsened.

'Right now? I have to come over? Okay. Where do you live again?' Jun forgot who he was speaking with halfway through. Or maybe he hadn't understood in the first place. He should have known exactly where Nobu lived. The phone call lasted ages. She wouldn't hang up. 'Yeah, I will. I'm on my way. Okay. You're there, right?'

I took the phone off Jun. 'Listen, Nobu, don't make things worse. What do you think'll happen if he goes out in this condition?'

'Don't you get on your high horse, wifey. He loves me way more than you.'

'That's great.' I laughed. I'd never intended to compete with this woman. Ridiculous. Couldn't stand it.

'What's wrong with you? Acting all relaxed! Laughing!'

'I'm not relaxed at all.' I was pretty glum. Jun sat with his knees up like a child. He looked uneasy.

'My family's a lot better off than yours. My dad runs a bank. If Jun married me, we could help him.'

Nobu's mum had phoned me up from far away and said the same thing. You too, she said, and you could bring the kid, how about it, a fresh start, you're still young. So, parents were encouraging their daughters' adulteries these days.

'Why are you telling me this? You all just do what you like anyway. What I want you to do is stop coming and staying in my house for weeks on end. I hate cooking your meals and picking up your underwear. And keep your hands off my child.' I exploded once I got into mother mode. No baby was responsible for its father's behaviour. This woman had no right to do anything to that child.

'Don't worry, I will. I only pinched it before like that because I can't stand crying babies.'

'Then don't come here!' As I put the phone down, I could hear her shrieking about something. I took a deep breath. I wasn't a particularly maternal type, but I knew that a baby's crying didn't give other people a license to lay their hands on it. Crying was what a baby did every day.

I looked up at the ceiling, thinking seriously about what to do. The phone rang. I didn't want the sound to agitate Jun so I picked the receiver up and put it back down straight away. It rang again. I hung up again. At this rate she might actually come over, I thought. That's the kind of woman Nobu was. I had an idea. I called up an acquaintance, Takei.

'Nobu won't let up. Can you get her to stop calling? And not come over uninvited? Jun's in a bad way, he's lost it.'

Takei was calm. He was quiet and composed even after I told him a little about Jun's condition. I felt some relief. He said he'd try to talk Nobu round.

Jun stood up. 'I need to go.'

'Where?'

'To Izumi's. I need to see her.'

'I'm Izumi, Jun.' I hadn't realised it was that bad.

'Don't lie to me.' He gave a thin laugh. 'You're Nobu, aren't you? Dressing up as Izumi to trick me.'

'Come on. Come here.' He acquiesced when I spoke more forcefully. I had him get completely undressed. So he wouldn't go outside while he was this crazy. I hid his clothes. Jun seemed confused. Even with his mind all messed up, he still knew he couldn't go out naked.

'I gotta go, gotta go.' He wrapped himself in a bedsheet.

'Where to?'

He considered the question. 'Where? Well, hey, where should I go?'

'You should stay here.'

'It's raining,' he said, huddling nearer to the windowsill.

I went into the kitchen. I should at least get him to eat something, I thought.

'Oh, here's my mother and my sister!'

I turned around. Jun was holding the baby out of the second-floor window. I ran over and took our child out of his hands.

147

'Why did you do that? They're here to see the baby. I was just about to hand over our . . .'

He stared at me up and down, the baby in my arms.

'Why, you're Izumi! Aren't you?'

Apparently seeing me combined with the child helped him figure it out.

'That's right.' I started crying unexpectedly.

'Where were you? You've been neglecting me.'

'No, Jun. You've been doing the neglecting.' The tears wouldn't stop. I soothed the baby.

The phone rang. I thought it'd be Takei but it was Nobu, screaming on the other end.

'Enough of your fucking dirty lies! Trying to keep me away!' She had no idea. 'Alright, fine, I'll allow you to be in charge tonight.' What was she thinking? 'In return, you're never to phone us or come over once I'm married to him! I'll let you off just this once!'

'Good, got it.' I wrapped the phone in a blanket and put it under the duvet.

Jun had returned to the corner of the room. 'Where am I?'

'How about something to eat?'

'I've got some eggs here in case I get hungry. I'm fine for now. Never thought I'd be living in a chicken coop like this, huh. So World War Three happened after all.'

I stared him in the face.

'Wait, why am I outside Kawasaki Station? That cop over there's just eyeballing me.'

'Jun,' I said.

'How do you know my name? We've only just met.' He was genuinely surprised.

'When did we meet?' I wanted to cry.

'About a week ago. And listen, you shouldn't be hanging around with guys at your age.' Scowling, he began to lecture me. 'You're only in your second year at middle school, you're still a child.'

I could hear the phone faintly through the bedding. It wouldn't stop ringing.

Jun didn't sleep for three days.

I was in a car being driven through Yokosuka's concrete streets. I was gazing absently out of the window, the baby in my arms. I was so tired I couldn't sense anything. I could've been sliced up or beaten to a pulp and I wouldn't have felt a thing.

Takei had put me in touch with a psychiatrist who worked at a clinic down on the Miura peninsula. It was a long way to go, but after talking it over we decided it was best. Nobu brought herself along, of course.

'It's National Cleaning Day today.' Jun was in good spirits, maybe because he could see the outside world from the car windows. 'Hey, apparently security guards get paid three times as much if they have to work out on the street.'

He was having a great time all by himself. I reckoned they'd have him committed.

'When we get to the clinic let me speak with the doctor alone, okay?' Nobu said, still oblivious. 'I know Jun best, after all.' Even now she wanted a power struggle.

'You stay with me.' Takei spoke very calmly, gripping the wheel. 'I won't be saying anything either. Only his wife needs to speak to them.'

Nobu went quiet, but she didn't look happy. No doubt she felt we were being nasty to her. Maybe she even thought I'd persuaded Takei to take my side. It was all so ridiculous that I wanted to just give up. It was too much. Why did I have to go through this? It seemed absurd and unreasonable no matter how I looked at it.

'Jun's very dependent on you,' Takei said to me.

'No he's not,' Nobu declared. 'I'm the one he depends on.'

'Right,' I agreed, 'it's not me he's dependent on.'

All because I submitted to him back then. And that was because (though it hurt to remember, it felt so long ago) Joel had dumped me. If only I hadn't been so impatient. If I could, I'd return to Honmoku back in the day. To before I'd met Jun.

'Hey, Jun,' I said. 'Don't hit me anymore, okay?'

'Okay, I won't.' He smiled grimly. 'What will I fill my days with, then?'

Still cracking jokes, even as the madness took full hold. But I wasn't surprised. I was too tired.

11

I've Got a Mind to Give Up Living

One day, I realised I was twenty-nine.

I stood by the kerb, dumbstruck. It was a paved shopping street facing the Kannana-Dori circular. I had a four-pack of toilet rolls in my right hand and my purse in my left. I was gazing at the buildings and the sky.

The sky was pale blue. I could see flecks of light like fine dust. They sparkled. The late-afternoon sun marked off the tops of the buildings and flattened the scenery into a two-dimensional picture. Several glass windows reflected a fierce, screeching light. The light shone clear and distinct. The spaces between the panes formed chains of crosses. One cross was particularly big and strong. I was captivated by the light. My mind had eased off. Then, slowly, I remembered. I'd felt an intense happiness in that stray moment.

I walked towards the apartment. A car passed by. Today wasn't a particularly lovely day or anything. It was just the first time in months I'd had a chance to look at the scenery around me. I'd been too absorbed with all that turmoil of mine.

The light beat strongly on the dirty pedestrian bridge, too. I felt joy and a heartbreaking sadness. Both came together and both gnawed at me mercilessly.

I endured it. What choice did I have. I actually preferred not being able to suppress it. Joy and misery pierced through me, violent, strong and without a cause. I thought I might start getting the shakes. I turned the corner and although the light was out of sight then, the feelings it instilled continued for a while. By the time I got home I was exhausted. I put down my shopping and sat on a chair in the kitchen. The misery-infused bliss finally subsided. I don't think I'd noticed the breeze, the light, the temperature for almost half a year. I was too deranged.

Jun was dead. The five years I'd spent with him felt like a hundred. Time stretched interminably when he was alive. As if we'd been together from before we'd both been born. And would stay together forever into the future. 'I had a dream,' he'd told me. 'We were standing on the shore, holding hands. The final war was over and most of humanity had died. Strange-shaped fish and shells had washed up at the water's edge. It was the future, but also just shortly after the Earth had been formed. Across the ocean we could see a rising mushroom cloud. The sky was scarlet red.'

It had been anything but normal. He got sectioned twice. There were times when he wouldn't stop hitting me. We were happy for two months after our Harajuku chapter. But because of his illness, I started hating it all again. The fights resumed and carried on for a long time. It was always dramatic. Jun's clothes (baggy *sukaman* trousers) and gestures were out of the early sixties, but his emotions were atavistic and violent. He seemed to believe that the entire truth of everything would become clear in a single, spectacular moment.

A year before he died he told me he loved me. He said he'd never been able to love any partner before. Not even the one who'd been killed by a car right before his eyes when he was twenty-one. I thought I just lacked the ability to love people, he said.

Everything had a whiff of the nineteenth century with Jun.

Oh, and let's not forget. He also experienced something almost identical to the regression that happened to me in Harajuku. Two weeks before he realised he loved me, Jun reverted to being Kawasaki's number-one bad boy. He started talking about his days spent fighting, taking drugs, gang-raping women – all as if it were yesterday. The words tumbled out mechanically. After a pause, he said the past decade was like a dream. These things were from very long ago, yet felt so fresh. As if the very same thing were happening all over again. When he fell asleep out of total exhaustion, he had a nightmare. He woke up yelling a name, Ryoji, Ryoji, why did they kill you? He could suddenly see a friend of his who'd been stabbed after some gang rumpus. Jun wept. Then he told me something he'd never admitted to anyone else. When he was sixteen, he killed someone. There was a fight and his adversary died the next day.

He seemed simpler than before, rather less intelligent. We lived in peace for a year. We were always together. There was no big upheaval. If he didn't know where I was for more than two hours, he'd report me as missing to the police. Then one day he died of an overdose. He was twenty-nine.

I had an abnormal marriage. Not because of the specifics of what happened. But because that period feels like it belongs to a separate temporal axis. As if I'd had a long bad dream. It occurred and concluded completely in that parallel world. Meaning it'll last forever.

Returning to myself like this now, I feel I was tricked. Not by Jun, but by some indescribable great force. My time was stolen. It became someone else's life. I mean, when I look back now it all seems like a lie.

I sat still on the kitchen chair until it was completely dark. When I tried to stand up, I stumbled, because my legs were numb (I'd had them crossed).

No one can stay insane. You can't survive. After Jun died I kept thinking of him, then loathing him, on repeat. I could never love him in the end. I decided to stop wasting energy on a grudge. I'd changed myself to live with him. Now I had to build myself up again. With only my own strength, too. Far from easy to do.

I opened a drawer and took out several airmail letters. I'd restore those five vacant, lost years in another way. Maybe I couldn't get them back. But I'd restore my twenty-four-year-old self. I poured some coffee into a big mug. I wanted to put one of my records on, but Jun had broken them all long ago. I switched on a light and faced the desk.

By now I should be in Tokyo, seeing you and the baby, but instead I'm here writing you a letter. I cancelled my plans to go to Japan. Partly because I heard the business with my apartment has already been settled, but mainly due to the state Pete's in, mentally and physically.

Now, Pete and I are separate people of course. Even if he's unwell, I'm still healthy and should be able to go anywhere, but when it actually comes down to it . . .

There's rarely much sense to what he says and does. His sense of time and money is very loose, by which I mean unreliable. When he goes out, he just stays out, and I have no idea where he is, what he's doing, or when he'll be back. Even when he does call me, he's always three or four hours later than he says he'll be. He's not only like this in his personal life – for the last six months especially, he's been that way with work, too.

Falling asleep during recordings, skipping rehearsals unannounced, not returning calls . . .

As you know, I'm a bit neurotic compared to most people. And this stays between you and me, but I got so tired of it all that I just took a load of sleeping pills. It didn't work, I didn't die. I wound up in hospital for a week after that. This was in early July.

When I got out I spoke with Eddie Henderson, the trumpeter (he also works as a psychiatrist). He said that Pete's the one who's unwell, not me.

Eddie's worked with Pete a few times and his opinion as a doctor had been that he should take some time out to rest, but only this time did he realise the extent of the problem. They were about to tour in Europe and right until a few days before departure Eddie was dead set against Pete going. But they couldn't find a new bassist at short notice, so Pete packed some tranquillisers and went in the end.

He could only get to sleep once every few days (he's been like that at home too, for the past two years). When he did sleep, he'd sweat litres and litres. Not only the sheets but the whole bed would be soaked. Because of his nerves.

And what's more, I'd been noticing for a while how fast we always ran out of money. We argued almost all year round about it, as well as about the loose time thing I mentioned. He was still buying weed and cocaine.

He smoked all day long in the house. I'd made a fuss about it before and tried to get him to stop, but it was no use so I shut up. I smoked too for a few months after I gave birth, because I had such bad moods, but I stopped. People say it's harmless but if something sucks your energy like that it can't be good.

I thought he'd stopped doing coke about a year ago but turns out he'd just been hiding it.

I reckon it's those things that helped Pete develop his loose attitude towards time and money.

I think it'll improve after what's happened now, but I still wasn't sure about going to Japan. I thought we might break up. I'd also lost my passport and the purse with my green card in it, so nothing was lining up right.

But it's helped me sort my feelings out. I've realised I need to rethink things before Pete gets back from Europe. He needs to do some thinking too.

If after that Pete still has the same attitude as before, then we'll break up once and for all.

I've Got a Mind to Give Up Living

All his friends agree that he's become a totally different person since he started playing with Herbie. I think they're right. It's the same with famous performers in Japan, it consumes you mentally and physically.

A tour, another tour, recording . . . He's had no chance to just relax at home these past two years. Even if he did get a week off, he can't just shake off his habits. His body's programmed to be rushing about. So even if there's nothing he has to do, he'll still rush about.

You've been much on my mind lately for some reason. I couldn't stop thinking of you. I had no idea about Jun. When I found out I couldn't help wondering if two women might always end up with the same fate if they have similar dispositions and live through the same time. Well, I suppose Pete never hits me and he does give me money to live. I also don't think we're as close-knit as you and Jun.

When he's away on tour I try to tug on my memory by reminiscing about Japan. I'll never be able to go back to who I was. The reason why I still don't leave is because I'm scared of stepping in a new direction. Even though it was far better being by myself.

Sometimes I feel like listening to Green Glass. For me (and even more for you, I imagine), Joel and Landi aren't just musicians I liked – they've become like symbols of my youth, as hammy as it is to say it like that. Makes me think of Foo, too. Wonder what happened to him.

Back then I had no idea how terrifying life could be. I just made decisions and ran with them headlong without thinking about the consequences, and this is the result. You and I are both at our wits' end.

Did you say you'd sent me Jun's record? I changed address, so they should forward it to me.

This letter is so long already. I can't keep losing myself in memories, so I'll leave it here. My kid's grown out of all these clothes, maybe I'll send them to you next week.

Alright, take care. Farewell.

That letter was the last I ever heard from Etsuko.

12

Keep Me Hangin' On

I was listening to the singles hit parade when the phone rang. I turned down the volume and picked up the receiver.

'Izumi, is that you?' Some guy's voice I didn't recognise.

'Yes, it is.'

'Baby,' sang Masahiko Kondo on the stereo. When things got a bit bluesy the word sounded more like 'babe-eh'. RC Succession did that unfailingly.

The guy on the phone gave his name. Joel. After a moment I found my voice and told him firmly that I was glad he'd called. He sounded hesitant.

'My heart's racing,' I said.

'What are you up to this minute?'

I thought I could hear a smile in his voice. He pronounced every word clearly and completely. Didn't drop any final syllables, those old shy habits gone now.

'I'm hanging some bedding out to dry.'

Matchy was singing something about being young now. I would never understand this song. No matter how many times I listened, the lyrics made no sense at all.

'Right then, do you fancy coming over?' He sounded happy.

'Where are you?'

'At home.'

'But what about your wife?'

'She's visiting family for the next three days.'

'You sound awfully pleased about that.'

'Sneaker Blues' was still playing. Something about fuzz guitar in the lyrics. But no actual fuzz guitar in the song. Fuzz pedals were no longer being produced, but you could get something similar with a distortion pedal. RC's 'Transistor Radio' was full of it.

'Got the day off today and tomorrow.' Joel was relaxed. Tsutsumi Kyohei's hit ended dramatically.

'So shall I come over? I've got a big bruise on my face which'll take me about an hour to cover up.' I'd fainted on the stairs in the subway station, and told him so.

'When did you do that?'

'Ninth of September.' The three-year anniversary of my husband's death. There was a memorial for Jun but I didn't go, because I hate jazz people. I knew they'd be all gloomy and mournful. Some people said it was punishment for having neglected him. I couldn't disagree more. After devoting myself to him that much, I'd rather be left to do as I please.

'Did you bruise your body too?' A strange question to ask.

'Yeah, here and there.'

'You'll have to show me everything.'

I shrieked and he laughed.

'Take the Toyoko Line from Shibuya down to Sakuragicho. It'll take you thirty-five minutes.' Joel's instructions were precise. Maybe he remembered I was late last time.

'Call me from the station. A taxi should cost about a thousand yen. Ask for the Honmoku-nichome bus stop, they'll know it.'

He always did like a bus stop.

'We're near Green Glass,' said the driver. The name of an old nightclub.

'He said he'd be waiting.'

'Is it this man here?'

'Couldn't say, my eyesight isn't great.'

He saw me through the window while the taxi was still moving. The window was rolled down slightly. 'Izumi?' he asked and pushed 1,500 yen through the gap. I paid the driver myself. Returned the two notes when I'd got out. The sun was shining faintly.

He was tall, skinny, wearing a plain jumper. Great big beard. I wasn't surprised by how much he'd changed because I'd seen him on TV the week before. It was quite a wide street. He'd started crossing over when the traffic lights changed.

'How come you remember me?'

'You've got a great body, we've got good chemistry.' He didn't beat around the bush. 'It felt really good with you back then so I've always remembered it. I wanted to do it again.'

He should've called up earlier! I wanted to snap my fingers. That said, I think I moved house as soon as I met Jun.

'I bet you forgot my face though.' I looked at him.

'Yeah, I did.' He looked me in the face again. 'Now I remember it.'

'I've aged since we last met.' I looked down. I was filled with emotion. It wasn't just simple misery.

'So have I. I'm thirty-three now. You're a year younger, right?'

We were so young when we met the first time. Middle-aged the second time. We weren't beautiful anymore, no longer a picture.

We'd crossed the road. It must have been around half four. Songwriters still wrote lyrics about Honmoku. Even though the place had become all rundown and deserted. The American off-base houses had disappeared, the colonial culture from there had been diluted and spread across the whole of Japan. Rumour was that urban planners wanted to turn the area into a park. You couldn't be sure of that, all the same. The streets of Honmoku would be gone. To think this place used to be one of Yokohama's two big draws, alongside Chinatown. Nowadays no one would particularly miss it.

We went down a smaller street lined with houses. Nothing flashy. Was he really taking me to his home? Normally you'd sort out somewhere else.

'You know my wife, right?'

'No.'

'You'd recognise her face. Remember Miyanaga? She used to go out with him.'

'Nope.'

We turned a corner. I changed the subject.

'Must be hard to make a living playing in bands.'

'It's tough.'

'My husband played solo. He's had five albums out since he died. I've not seen a cent of any royalties.'

'I've never got any royalties. When I stopped playing with Green Glass, the label actually took two hundred thirty thousand yen off me.'

We arrived at a two-storey house. His mother's name was written in huge script on the doorplate. His own and one other name were written in smaller script, slightly further away. It was just a two-minute walk from the venue where they'd held their debut show, fifteen years ago.

A bunch of white dogs flew over to us as soon as he opened the door. I stiffened and stepped backwards. When I was fifteen a dog bit my arm. The wound was deep, and I still had a scar. Since Jun's death I was even scared of cats. This fear of living creatures had begun since I'd felt close to death.

'Don't worry, they won't bite.' Joel fended them away from me. Four Maltese dogs.

He placed his hand on my back and ushered me up the stairs. The dogs followed. In a room at the top of the stairs was a woman who must have been his mother. I gave her an awkward wave. Joel opened the door to another room and let me enter first. He locked the door behind us with his other hand. We were in a kitchen, which led to a bedroom. A married couple lived here. If he's locking the door and we're together in here, I thought, then his mother must surely know. Why else would he bring a girl in here? He didn't seem bothered.

There was a sofa and a double bed. In the middle was a table with a pyramid-shaped lamp on top. There was a wooden floor, no carpet. Joel sat me down on the bed. He stood there and said, 'You're staying the night, right?' How brazen.

'My wife's family lives in Isogo,' he added. So, just a stone's throw away on the Negishi Line.

I'm a pretty decisive type. Men are never as bold as me. They're too cautious and timid. Even Jun was the more cowardly of us two. But Joel was unique. I'd never met someone who took so few precautions. It went beyond naivety and into recklessness.

'Things weren't going so well with Miyanaga and she suddenly came to Kyoto.' He started telling me how they got married.

'Was this after you spoke to me on the phone?'

He nodded. 'She lives really nearby so she'd come over a lot. Gradually she stayed overnight more and more. After we'd been living together for two years, we made it official.'

So, that was one way of doing it. I should've clung onto him too.

'It's been six years now. I've not cheated on her once. She even comes with me to work. That level of surveillance isn't normal.'

Still, he seemed resigned to his fate. He sat down on the floor.

'She's a Taurus, which is why she wants me all for herself.'

'My husband was the same sign.'

'Bet he'd get really jealous, right?'

'Like jealousy incarnate. He was insane, sure, but with our relationship he managed to focus all of his energy into restricting my freedom. Always wanted us to be together. Made me

164

come to all his gigs. The last thing you want to see is your husband performing on stage.'

Joel laughed. He'd been grinning for a while. 'When we're together we do it all the time. She goes quite wild sometimes. Seems like sex is my thing. I'm a Scorpio, so I'm ruled by Pluto.'

'Different than when you were younger?' We were now both old enough to have this conversation.

'All the stronger, lately . . .' He took a pack of Mild Sevens from the table. 'The world's tough, isn't it? When I'm not working I just want to forget. That's why I get so into it.'

I was fidgeting, restless. I'd been amped up since getting on the Toyoko Line. As Joel was smoking, I got some cigarettes from my bag. I tried to take one out of the box but my hands were shaking and I dropped it. Joel noticed and asked if I wanted a tranquilliser. Just like the old days. He was so attentive, but in his own way.

'Yes,' I said. I didn't want to snub his goodwill. He opened a flat square tin like a box of crackers. Filled with all sorts of pharmaceuticals.

'Strong one? Weak one?' A lesson in hosting from a seasoned self-medicator.

'Weak.' Solicitously he placed two white pills in my palm. Fetched me some water too. I swallowed them down.

'Should we go to a hotel?'

Why would he even ask that? I knew he didn't have any money. Musicians are always skint. I didn't feel great about him asking his mother for 10,000 yen or whatever for the room, either.

'Don't mind either way,' I replied.

'Me neither.'

The phone rang. Joel left the room and went to the phone by the stairs. I looked around while smoking a cigarette. I remembered reading an article with a headline like 'We Just Visited Heartthrob Joel at His Home!' in an early issue of *An-An*. Talked about how he had all these objects everywhere, as if he had a phobia of empty space. His current place wasn't anything like that. Maybe his wife's doing.

Joel came back.

'You'll eat something, right? I ordered food from the Chinese place nearby. And let's have some tea.'

I followed him into the kitchen. Looked around the shelves and found some Chinese tea. There were sheets of newspaper spread on the floor around the sink. I guessed he'd spilled something while his wife was away and this was as far as he'd made it with the clean-up. My hands hadn't stopped shaking. I boiled the kettle and made the tea, with difficulty. Everything I held shook and made a racket.

'Chinese tea's good for you,' he explained. 'Flushes out the toxins.'

Habitual drug users have this strange practice. No qualms about poisoning themselves relentlessly, yet extremely concerned with healthy living. Jun was the same. Doped up to his eyeballs half the time but still bought a health magazine called *Sokai* every month. They can't stop themselves buying any books they see with titles like *Your Wholegrain Revolution*, *Fasting for Health*, *The Wonders of Tai Chi*, *Yoga Yourself Younger*. Not that they ever put any of it into practice. Maybe it's more about restoring a kind of psychological balance.

'Let's have it chilled.'

He was looking at me.

'Don't you ever cook?' I asked.

'No,' he said.

Not that I cared. It wasn't as if we were married. I poured the tea into a plastic jug and put it in the fridge door. I wasn't wearing slippers. My toes were on show.

'Let me tell you something that'll put you off.' Maybe best said earlier rather than later. 'I don't have a little toe on my left foot. My husband cut it off with a kitchen knife three months after we met.'

The look on Joel's face slowly changed. 'That must've hurt so much!' He was frowning.

'It did. I'll show you.'

We went back to the sofa in the bedroom and I took off my tights. I showed him my foot. He took a long look.

'Jesus. Why did he do that?'

'He wanted me all for himself. He didn't want any other man to have me. There's something wrong with that kind of love, isn't there?'

Joel kept shaking his head in disbelief. He went quiet, then began: 'I've never fucked a virgin. Even when girls were throwing themselves at me, I'd always ask if they'd had sex before first. If not, I wouldn't do it. I'd feel so bad about seeing them in pain.'

He said nothing more for a while. If only I'd understood him better, back then. If only I'd known he liked me. If only I'd pursued him a little harder. If I'd been with Joel, first of all my body probably wouldn't be scarred like this.

'She said it was her first time, but didn't seem like it hurt at all.' As if he was talking to himself.

I suddenly realised something. 'Your wife, did she use to live in Yoyogi-Uehara?'

'Yeah.'

'And went to art school?'

'That's right.'

So it was Yuka! And Sleeve Man's real name was Miyanaga.

'When she was putting us in touch she called me and said, "I'm sending a girl your way, she's got a great body." Then I met you, and she was right.'

Joel wasn't embarrassed at all. He spoke quite calmly.

'It's been a while since I've seen someone else's body like this. It's pretty arousing.'

I was wearing a cream satin shirt beneath a black suit. He went on, 'You dress so seductively. Flashy looks don't really do it for me. Yuka likes dressing all loud and showy. She's a bit of a princess. Can't stop herself if she sees something she wants.'

'I gather she's on good terms with your mother, on the surface.'

'Yeah, on the surface.'

'Do you love her?'

'Yeah, I love her, let's say that I love her.' His response was calm.

'Hey, what's love?'

'This, surely?' He reached out and placed his hand on my crotch before immediately taking it away.

'Maybe I didn't love Jun after all, then. I don't remember it ever being really good with him.'

168

We were never a good match sexually. And his sadistic side came out more and more. I kept rejecting it, so he'd have to satisfy those urges with other girls. I decided the reason he needed to bully women so much was some major insecurity about his own manhood. He had a complex about his looks, too. I'm sure his life would have been very different if he'd been taller.

'And did he want it a lot?'

'He was like a male nymphomaniac. I knew women could be that way, but I'd never seen it in a man. He came eleven times in a day once. I told him I'd had enough, but no dice. By the eighth time he was in pain himself. He said it was like a religious penance, the more he fucked the holier he became. This was at age twenty-four.'

Joel opened his brown eyes even wider. Those eyes alone hadn't changed.

'He must've been on something,' Joel said decisively. 'No one can come that many times normally.'

'And six times the day after. It wasn't fun at all.'

Only that Harajuku dusk could move me. I found sex to be more in the mind.

'It's hard to believe you spent so long with someone like that.'

'I know. Well, I managed to bear it. It's a defect of mine, I know, but if someone's pushy enough I always cave in. Even if I absolutely hate it, I'll just let myself be dragged along. My mother was cold and controlling with me. Even now, as an adult, I'm just repeating that relationship. I'm always subservient. So are you, right?' I looked up at Joel.

'Subser-what?' he asked innocently.

'You know, passive and . . .'

'Oh, got you.' He laughed. 'So I've learned a new word today.'

I gazed at him. What a sweet-natured guy. Maybe he picked up that I was touched.

'Listen, I'm not into foreplay. Guys usually take a girl for a drink or whatever, right? They enjoy the chase, the seduction. That's not me, not at all. With me you're either in or you're not. And I know what I want: not just anyone will do. Unless she's got a tight waist and round hips, I'm out. I haven't even slept with that many girls. Under a hundred. First time was in my last year of high school.'

'Pretty late for a kid playing in bands.'

'That time I picked four groupies who fit my type and we each fucked like that, one after the other.'

'Hordes of girls must've been throwing themselves at you.'

'Yep. It got to a point when just the idea of more women made me feel sick, and I didn't touch anyone for a whole year. I was always running away from them. This was before we met, by the way.'

He looked at my body. 'But I like women now. They're warm, and I can have sex with them.'

I reached out and touched his neck. He stroked my thighs.

'You were wearing this stiff girdle before.'

He was running through whatever he could remember. I'd completely forgotten whether I was wearing a girdle or not.

'Your hair down there was pretty sparse, I think.'

I was impressed that he remembered such things. Yet he'd forgotten what my face looked like. Not many men remembered the quirks of my body more than my face.

'I remember thinking you had this tight waist. Men love your kind of figure. Bet loads of guys hit on you, huh?'

'They did. Lots.' I smirked, mouth closed.

'And you fucked them, right? Lots?' Joel got closer.

'Yep.' I smiled, mouth open, baring my teeth. He reached over. I stood up and he rose to meet me and we held each other. His face was higher than the top of my head. I like taller men. Feels reassuring. I was young again. I let the trance take over my body. His hands moved behind my waist, lifting my skirt bit by bit, revealing my underwear. When I realised, I turned around. There was a dresser behind me. He was watching us in the mirror.

'Your legs . . .', he said, always noting and detailing.

I moved away from him. My face was flushed. I pulled my skirt back down. Then I clung to him violently. He gently loosened my arms. Lightly patted my back, like he was soothing me.

'After dark, okay? We've got relatives visiting downstairs. Sound travels in shabby digs like this, the place is basically made of cardboard.'

Digs. Hadn't heard that word in a while.

'My mother's sister lives with her husband in the other bit of the house. They don't have any kids, but still. And my uncle's visiting, so we can't make any noise.'

I quickly undid the buttons on my blouse regardless, and he gave me another once-over.

'That's a cute bra. Show me what you've got on below.'

I took off my skirt. 'Cute,' he said again. My underwear wasn't cute at all. I was wearing some plain, grown-up shorts. Deep purple.

Joel touched my breasts. He was testing what they felt like. 'Lovely. Very smooth.' He moved away slightly and took a look. 'You've got such fine, fair skin.' All men said this. He stood up and opened a built-in closet. 'Put some clothes on for now. Not that anyone's likely to come in, but you know.' He brought out some women's clothing. 'Yuka left these behind.'

'You make it sound like you've split up.'

'Oh, you think?'

Joel selected a red negligee. What on earth was he thinking? He had some nerve. Yet I did as I was told, just as when he had offered me the tranquillisers. I put on his wife's clothes. Something was wrong with me too.

The phone rang several times. He duly answered each call while I sat on the bed. It was dark now. He wasn't coming onto me at all. I was getting frustrated. He came back and put the television on.

'I prefer to take it easy when I have time off. Empty my mind and look at the screen. You're all about speed,' he looked at me, 'and so am I.'

We both lay down on the bed. We watched *Yan-Yan Singing Studio*.

'How about Matsuda Seiko?' I asked, as we watched her sing on the screen.

'Sure, I'd screw her.'

'I didn't expect your cousin and his pal would be there that time.'

'Neither did I.'

'You didn't seem to be too into it.'

'Well, we weren't alone.'

I was getting more and more frustrated. I flung myself at his skinny body. 'I can't wait any longer.' I'd been dreaming about it for so long already.

'But the food's coming.' Joel tried to calm me down. I shook my head and rubbed his chest through his jumper. He took my hand and put it on top of the bulge in his trousers.

'Come on,' I said.

'Okay. Just a little.'

He took off his jumper and shirt. He took off his brick-red trousers. This time he was wearing white underwear. He was upright on his knees on the bed. He took out his penis. He drew my head closer. I couldn't quite get it into my mouth. It was too big. I used my hand.

He said, 'I'm close,' and pulled away. He took off his underwear and fetched a condom. I tried to put it on him but it was useless, my hands were shaking too much. I was so excited.

'Shit! I can't do it.' I sounded like I was at the end of my tether, and I was.

'Is it the drugs?' He seemed to think I was having withdrawal symptoms. No, it's *you*. But I couldn't bring myself to say that. I didn't want to flatter him. He helped me slowly out of my underwear. The shakes had spread across my whole body. There was no way I could shed my clothes swiftly without help.

'What's this?' He touched one of the scars on my wrist.

I groaned. 'It's where he put out his cigarettes. Come on, don't make me remember.'

I covered my face with both hands. I could sense a thick, gloopy loathing stirring. I felt sick.

'Sorry,' he said. He took my hands. 'Don't cry.'

The pop music show was still going on the TV.

'Turn the lights off,' I requested quietly. Playing up this shy-girl act all of a sudden. He got up from the bed and flicked the wall switch. The ceiling lights went out. Then he turned on a bedside lamp.

'No, please.'

'I want to see you.' Joel was on all fours on the bed.

'No.'

'Open your legs for me.' He lowered his head and tried to see that part of me.

'No, I've had a baby . . .'

'It's fine,' he said. He placed his hands on my thighs. He wasn't forcing me. I brought my legs together and stretched them out straight. I felt bad about it, but I tried asking him to stop.

'I can't get in unless you open your legs, can I?' Reasonable.

I opened my legs slightly, careful not to let anything be visible. He gave up on trying to see and moved his thin body upwards on top of me. He went in. He was big. I sighed quite audibly. I felt him so much I almost couldn't believe it.

'Try not to make much noise,' he whispered.

He moved slowly, to keep me calm. I could barely stand it. I'd dreamt for so long of meeting him again, being held by him once more. He embodied my youth. He was the symbol of a vanished time. I couldn't let it go. The more terrifying life became, the stronger he shone within me.

Joel probably didn't know how much he meant, but his lack of bother made him all the more beautiful. I put my arms around his torso. He was skinny. About the same as before. Then it came on me suddenly. I spasmed. His thrusts were gentle. I got close again.

'Did you just come twice?' He looked at me face-to-face.

'No, not a second time, not yet.' My voice was gravelly. All the excitement had made my throat go funny. He held me in his lanky arms and sank into me again. I shook my head. 'That feels good, feels good.'

His penis left no room inside me, he was hefty and I was full. It didn't match his delicate outward appearance. Seemed like a capacity upgrade to me.

'I love you.'

I finally said it. Back then – when Etsuko and I were frolicking through the night, when the world wore such an unreal sheen, when my energy was never crushed by my dreams no matter how vast they were – back then, I just couldn't say the word 'love'. My feelings were so outsized that I couldn't easily say it.

'You love this?' He asked the question flatly.

'You,' I said, 'I love you.' I clung to his neck. I came like that, clinging.

Joel stopped. He'd satisfied me enough.

'Didn't you feel it?' I felt abashed. It was like I'd been the only one enjoying it.

'No, it was great.' He was trying to make me feel better. 'Just that everyone's still awake, I couldn't get my mind off that.' As always. This was our fate. 'Hey, let's do it again later, okay? Properly.' He moved away slowly.

'Was I loud? I did try to be quiet.'

'Not really. I don't think anyone heard.'

'I couldn't feel anything when we did it before.'

'Right.'

'Maybe I've matured? Being married and all that.'

My time with Jun now felt like a long preparation for my reunion with Joel. I'd thought that as my husband he possessed me entirely. He'd created a woman, curated and moulded her for his own use. I wasn't wrong. Jun did want me, he wanted me no matter what. His needs were frightening. I catered to them. I even tried to provide what I didn't have. Among the things I had given him were my unfading girlish dreams. I don't think he ever knew how much Joel meant to me. He crunched up and swallowed down my feelings without ever understanding them. Your skin, your hair, your lips are all mine, he had said. He might have had an inkling, but just didn't want to acknowledge it. I could give him everything, and yet nothing could be done to erase my inner landscape.

Joel put his clothes on. He sat on the sofa. I put on my bra and panties. I couldn't stand. I was paralysed.

'You must've slept with all sorts of guys since we last met.' He wasn't criticising. He was reminiscing about the time that had passed.

'Girls, too.' I smiled.

'What do lesbians do?' He seemed interested.

'This and that.'

'Do you do "this and that" too?'

'I just go with the flow.'

'I'll get more out of you later.'

We were waiting for the night to thicken.

He left the room and brought back three plates of Chinese food. I'd had a headache for a while. I hadn't taken a bath in three days because I'd caught a cold. When Joel asked me over, I had simply wiped my body down and applied perfume.

'You got any painkillers?' I asked because I assumed he'd have plenty. Joel took the tin from before and picked out two bags of white powder. He told me what the drug was called but I didn't recognise the name. It was packaged as if it came from a clinic.

'This one's a gram. It'll take care of even severe pain. But I think a half-gram should be enough. You need to eat something first, though, or it'll mess up your stomach.'

I ate a steamed bun. It was filled with minced meat, bamboo shoots and mushrooms.

'Have some more.' He wasn't eating. He was watching me. 'I'm just overwhelmed at the sight of you.'

I blushed and laughed.

'What a line,' we both said at the same time.

Joel looked pleased. 'We just harmonised, huh.'

'Do you ever see Landi?' Chinese food always made me think of him.

'He's kept on with the restaurant. Even opened a second branch. He started playing again last year or so. Planning to put out a solo single, he says. We've not talked about Green Glass much lately but we're on good terms.'

'I heard he got divorced, right?'

'His wife went to the States with the kids. That was last year. He was pretty down for a while. He's a family man.'

I knew that. I sat on the floor in front of the sofa to listen.

'His wife needs to be Chinese. Think of the relatives. All it takes is for someone to tell the kids that their grandparents were killed by the Japanese.' Joel thought for a while. 'I'm glad we got less popular. Back then people always stared at us no matter where we went. I hate being stared at.'

Because he was mixed. Then, when he turned introverted and just played music, there was even more of a fuss. Which was the last thing he'd wanted.

'When I was eighteen I was reading a tabloid at a friend's place, and there was a memoir section by a girl who'd worked her way round the members of Green Glass.'

It was so far in the past, felt like a century ago. I read the piece when I was staying over with the first man I slept with after leaving high school.

'Oh, that.' Joel handed me a cushion. 'She was involved with gangs in Shinjuku. Did it for the money. But it was all true, you know. What was written.'

I had expected denial, so it was strange to hear this silly article treated with candour and seriousness.

'We didn't act coy like other bands. We didn't try to hide anything, we just behaved ... naturally. And for that they called us rough.'

'There'd never been a Japanese band with a bad-boy image before. I liked it. No problem.'

'Right?'

'After I slept with you, my friend said it was a good job I didn't catch anything.'

I meant that as a joke. Joel took it at face value.

'Probably because I was on solvents, I was all like this.' He slackened his jaw and stuck out his tongue. 'I was crazy. People started bitching and saying I had syphilis. I went to a mental hospital, you know.'

'I know.' Jun was admitted twice, too. I didn't think mentally ill people were freaks. I read tons of Freud in my first term at high school. I'd have got stuck into him earlier, but my middle-school library didn't have a psychoanalysis section.

'I . . .' I felt a bit sad. I looked into his eyes. 'Did you know how I felt about you?'

'No,' he answered gravely.

'I've always been in love with you, for years and years.'

'I thought you'd met up with me so you could write about it in a book.'

I almost couldn't breathe. So he knew. The year after I met Joel I'd written a short story called 'Honmoku Blues' for a literary magazine called Shosetsu Gendai. He knew he'd been used. How did he still look so calm?

'I'm glad you liked me,' he said.

The dogs barked outside the kitchen. Joel went to open the door.

'If you're wondering why I moved back here,' he said softly as he went back to the sofa, 'it's because of these rascals.' He pointed to the dogs following him about. He thought quietly for a moment before adding, in a muted voice: 'That's all.'

He was a dead man still living, on and on.

'Are they all females?'

'Yep. I put nappies on them when they get their periods. Gets a bit stinky when all four are in heat at once.' He picked up one of the dogs. 'This one was born premature. I fed her milk myself as she grew up.'

Joel was so lonely. Perhaps he didn't realise it himself. But he did recognise his situation. He'd given up hope and accepted things as they were.

Jun couldn't recognise it. Jun had to be with someone all the time. If that someone was a woman, he had to have sex with her. His actions were always compulsive. When Jun was with someone who actually mattered to him, it didn't make him happy at all. He was always running away. In the end he fled too deeply into the delusion of love and got lost. I wonder if he knew I didn't love him. I can't remember now what I got from him. I probably gave a great deal more than I ever received. All his energy went on shackling his wife down. Jun wasn't ungenerous, he just didn't know how to give.

The phone rang. Joel left the room again. I put on my own clothes. I left Yuka's red gown on the sofa. I lay face-down on the bed and stayed still.

Joel was back. I saw him slumped on the sofa out of the corner of my eye. He let out a long sigh but didn't say anything.

The room shook. It was a small earthquake. I lifted my head. He still said nothing. Just sat motionless in the same posture. I grabbed a pillow and buried my face again. I was so exhausted. I didn't move. The tremor stopped. After a while Joel came closer. He stood beside the bed. He gently tapped my shoulder several times.

'What's up?' He sounded even gloomier than before.

'I was just waiting quietly.'

'That was Yuka on the phone. She said she'd be here by eleven tonight to fetch something. And she's going to stay the night.'

I got up. It was almost ten o'clock. My headache had been beginning to subside but now I felt it worsening. I straightened my skirt and picked up my tights from the floor.

'This always happens when we meet. Someone gets in the way.'

'Yeah. I never imagined my cousin and his pal would be there that time before, either. Seems like that's my fate with you. Are you alright going back to Tokyo now?'

'What else would I do?' I pulled my tights on. I was in a bad mood.

Joel stuffed a few steamed buns into my black vinyl handbag.

'You can smell my perfume on the bedsheets.'

'It's fine, Yuka doesn't wash the sheets.'

I looked at him in surprise. He'd been confused when I told him on the phone earlier that I was hanging up bedding to dry. Did Yuka not do stuff like that?

'My mum does it for us when she's doing the rest of the laundry. Yuka never wants to leave my side. She's fallen pregnant three times now – had three abortions. Says we don't need kids.'

'The way she's attached to you seems exactly the same as Jun was to me.' So that's one way of doing love. I'd want to do it that way too, if I could. Tie up and fasten down a person I was obsessed with.

'We can't escape. Everything's already decided for us, right from the start.' Joel was committed to fatalism. Well, it wasn't such an impossible idea.

'But she'll be sleeping here tonight, won't she?'

'We had people over to play mahjong and one took a nap in the bed. Since there are relatives staying downstairs. I'll just say that's where the cigarette butts came from.'

I fixed my makeup. Joel fetched his wallet and opened it in front of me. 'For the taxi.' He took out 4,000 yen and handed it over. I happened to see that the 4,000 yen was all there was inside his wallet. He gave it all to me. We went down the stairs together. Our shoes were neatly lined up in the porch. I remembered just kicking them off anywhere when we arrived at the house. It was completely dark outside. Joel hugged me by the front door.

'I'll call you around one or two tomorrow. Yuka will be back at her family's place.'

I craned my neck up but could not reach his lips. He stooped and kissed me. He felt my waist once more. I walked alone to the main street. I felt melancholic. The night was thick in Yokohama.

13

Please, Time Machine

I was walking through Chinatown with her.

'And you haven't seen Joel since?' She stopped outside a wickerwork shop hung with baskets of all shapes and sizes.

'No.'

'Not even phoned him?'

'No.' That chapter had been closed, finally. After a decade.

She moved on. Big steamed buns were on display in a glass case. Hundred and seventy yen for a cold one. Two hundred and ten for one served hot. Chinese folk don't warm things up for free.

'That's Landi's place, you know.' Featured in a foodie-tour guidebook somewhere, no doubt. Another branch had been opened beside the Chinatown bridge.

'I heard his new stuff on TV. Blues songs set in Yokohama.'

She was twenty-one and living in Yokohama. This town's golden era was before her time.

'A month after I saw Joel, I met with Landi for work, for an interview. Strange how those two come as a pair for me. I was

the first person that each of them cheated on their wives with.'
I smiled faintly.

'Did Landi remember you?'

'He actually talked about how we'd slept together in front of my editor and the camera crew. I was pretty surprised. He must've been nervous. Wanted to get it in there first, before any damage was caused. He'd gained weight. He said himself that he'd gone downhill, that he was just a boring old man now.'

The shopfronts, bright in the afternoon light, looked like they'd been polished with oil. Even Chinatown was no longer sordid or filthy. All the buildings were tidy, all the businesses neatly packed in. We left through the gate near the seaside, onto a main street. The sun shone across the whole road. We waited for the lights to change.

'Has Joel given up?' she asked.

'Seems like it.'

'Why?'

'He probably reached some realisations too early on in his life, while he was still in his teens. That people have got to keep on living, even with nothing to hope for. That there's no such thing as absolute truth.'

'D'you think Jun realised all that as well?'

'Probably, but I'm not sure. If he did, it would've been in the year before he died.'

'If only he'd known sooner,' she said gently. 'Life could have been a lot more peaceful.'

Smart kid. Not that being smart will be useful for anything much. But that's okay, who cares if it's not useful.

'Unlikely, when you have that much passion. I feel like he lived in the wrong era. Maybe it's good he died, he's able to be at peace.'

We crossed the street and walked towards the oceanfront.

'What about Joel?'

'His era has passed. That might be one reason why he's given up. But it's not clear to me.'

'Presumably it's not clear to him either, right?'

'Right.' Maybe I shouldn't have been pouring this out to her. All I was saying was how, at last, my youth had ended. Youth has just begun for her. Her zest for life should be at its peak. A burning desire for tomorrow, all that.

We crossed the seaside promenade and went into Yamashita Park. People were strolling, stopping, chatting. The sunlight was bright and transparent. Someone was selling ice lollies. We sat down on one of the benches facing the ocean. There were seagulls flying high.

'Would you want to live your life over again?' she asked me, still facing forwards.

'If I could.'

She probably wouldn't understand. Doesn't matter. She'll probably live through a more troubled era than mine. A smooth, blank, fever-free age.

Some things you only understand once you've tried living. By the time you understand them, it's too late. That's in fact the reason why – no, I don't have the spirit to say that's what makes life spectacular. If I had enough initiative for that, then I wouldn't have gone through what I did. It feels like a punishment for my lack of courage. Even so, it's excessively cruel. Way out of proportion. For now, I accept the absurdity. Joel's the same. Jun couldn't accept it and now he's dead. He took a stand against life and time with all his might.

'I wonder what it all meant,' she said quietly. I knew what she was saying.

'Joel still has a beautiful heart, even though he's lost all hope. It's because he's completely given up, resigned completely. Whereas I still had some lingering attachment and regret – but not to him, I don't mean to him.'

'I know.'

'Attachment to the idea that my life could've been different. Meeting him again only stirred up that regret. Turns out he hadn't rejected me at all. But something else struck me, seeing how he lives now. We shouldn't grieve over what regret can't change.'

'It's a sad story.'

She turned to me. Her face was round, with beautifully fine, fair skin. It looked like she'd curled her eyelashes. Why couldn't time stop here? She could keep this loveable face forever. Nothing could harm her. Seeing people age is the hardest thing.

'It'll be summer soon.'

She gazed at the ships anchored in the harbour. Seagulls swooped between each vessel. The sunlight was being diffused by a light cover of cloud.

'I wish they'd blow a foghorn, even though there's no fog today.'

We sat side by side, watching the ships for a while.